STRAYS
LIKE US

Also by Cecilia Galante

The World from Up Here
Stealing Our Way Home

ALANTE

STRAYS LIKE US

Scholastic Press/New York

Library of Congress Cataloging-in-Publication Data available

ISBN 978-1-338-04300-6

10 9 8 7 6 5 4 3 2 1   18 19 20 21 22

Printed in the U.S.A.   23
First edition, July 2018
Book design by Nina Goffi

THIS ONE IS FOR JUDY, WHO ALWAYS LISTENS.

CHAPTER 1

I heard the barking right away, the noise of it carrying over the wind like a lost kite.

It was an urgent, frantic sound, and even though it was coming from behind a fence that cut through the yard of my new foster home and I was still on the back of Margery's motorcycle with my helmet squished down tight over my ears, I could hear the desperateness behind it. If barks could be turned into words, these might have said something like: "I-know-you're-there-and-you-can-hear-me-so-why-aren't-you-answering-why-won't-anyone-please-just-answer-me?"

Margery slowed the motorcycle to a stop, switched off the engine, and pulled off her helmet. "Don't mind him," she said. "That's the neighbor's dog. He gets a little worked up whenever he hears someone over here." She ran a hand over the top of her head, smoothing down the stray hairs, and swung her leg over the seat. "He'll settle down eventually. Come on inside. It won't be so loud in the house."

The dog kept barking.

I didn't move.

I had no idea what my short-term plan was just yet, but I was pretty sure it didn't include going inside. At least not yet. Margery Dawson, who some dumb caseworker at the Philadelphia Children and Youth Services center had decided would take care of me for the next few weeks or months or however long it was going to take, and who I'd known for exactly two hours and twenty-six minutes, hadn't *seemed* like someone who would tie me up and throw me down her basement steps, but then she didn't look like someone who drove around on a motor-cycle, either.

I thought she was kidding when we left the Children and Youth building and she walked over to the red-and-black Harley-Davidson in the parking lot—until she held out a shiny blue helmet and told me to hop on. I didn't take the helmet. I didn't do anything, really, except just stare at the bike for a minute. It was huge, with orange flames painted on the sides and all sorts of shiny dials on the front. The tires were as thick around as a man's arm, and the silver handlebars gleamed.

"You ever ride a motorcycle before?" Margery asked. It was the first thing she'd said to me besides "Hi, I'm Margery" inside the Children and Youth office.

I shook my head.

"Well, you don't have a thing to worry about. I've been riding Luke Jackson here for twenty years. He doesn't do anything without my permission."

"Luke Jackson?" I repeated.

"That's what I call him." She reached out and patted the seat. "After one of my favorite movie characters."

"What movie?"

"*Cool Hand Luke*. You ever hear of it?"

I shook my head.

"It's an old one. 'Bout a guy who goes to prison and works on a chain gang." She nudged the helmet at me. "Here. Put this on. And then sit back and enjoy the ride."

I was glad I was wearing a helmet. I was gladder still that I was sitting behind Margery so that she couldn't see the look of terror on my face as she gunned Luke Jackson's engine and sped out of the parking lot. I wasn't sure if I was more frightened of the motorcycle itself or the fact that she'd named it after some guy in prison, but it took me a good ten minutes to open my eyes, and another half hour to finally start breathing normally again. But by the time we passed the sign for Lancaster, and Margery rounded another bend, I realized she'd been right. She knew exactly what she was doing. And, man, she did it well.

"You coming?" Margery turned around now, her helmet tucked under one arm. Her khaki pants, denim shirt with white buttons down the front, and heavy work boots reminded me of a construction worker. She had a man's face, too, with rough, weathered skin and a large nose. Carmella, the caseworker at Children and Youth Services, had told me at least twenty-five things about Margery, including what she did for a living, but the only thing I'd remembered was the part about her never having had a foster kid before. I was her first. I'd blinked when she said that. Wondered if such a thing would turn out to be very, very good. Or very, very bad.

"Winifred?" Margery asked. "You want to come in now?"

I shook my head and stared at a large tree with yellow leaves, behind the fence. The dog's barking got louder. I wondered if he was under the tree, straining against some kind of leash. More likely, he was racing around the trunk, making himself dizzy.

"Okay, then." Margery spoke a little louder over the noise. "I'm not going to force you. There's not much to do out here, though. And it's going to get cold soon. You want me to bring you a jacket?"

I shook my head again.

"Suit yourself. I'll be inside when you're ready."

I listened to the sound of her boots crunching against the gravel behind me, and then the heavy thud of them as she made her way up her porch steps. My neck was sweaty, and the tips of my ears felt numb. The helmet was as big as a bowling ball and almost as heavy. I wondered if Darth Vader felt this way inside his: hot, stiff, and slightly claustrophobic. I pulled it off and rubbed my ears for a moment, trying to piece together all the things that had happened since this morning. But it was impossible. Every thought I had was interrupted by another bark.

Called out of science class by the principal—**BARK!**

Some lady from Children and Youth Services in there—**BARK!**

"Have a seat, Fred."—**BARK!**

"There's been an incident."— **BARK!**

"Yes, with your mother."—**BARK!**

"You'll have to come with me now, Fred."—**BARK! BARK! BARK! BARK! BARK! BARK! BARK! BARK! BARK! BARK! BARK!**

"Shut up!" I screamed, hurling the motorcycle helmet into the grass. "Shut up, shut up, shut *up*!"

A high-pitched whimpering sounded behind the fence, as if the dog had just dodged something heavier than my words. For a moment, everything was still. The only sound was the wind gusting through the yellow leaves. I slid off the bike slowly, taking care not to bump the shiny sides.

Just like that, the barking started again. It was even more desperate than before, almost pleading: "I-know-I'm-annoying-and-that-you're-already-angry-but-I-also-know-you're-still-there-please-come-talk-to-me-please."

"Man." I walked over and picked up the helmet. "You just don't give up, do you?" I headed toward the back of the fence, where the barks were coming from. Maybe the dog would settle down if I said a few words to him or let him lick my hand. I'd do anything to get him to be quiet. My head hurt, and my ears were starting to ring.

The fence was just high enough to prevent me from seeing over the top of it, but some of the slats along the bottom were rotted away. I knelt down next to one of the wider openings and peeked through.

For a split second, I wasn't exactly sure what I was looking at. It was definitely a dog, but I'd never seen a dog that looked so awful. Or so sad. He was smaller than I imagined he'd be, and his fur, which was so dirty that it hung in matted clumps against his body, seemed to be mostly black and white. Parts of his neck were rubbed raw where the metal links of a chain had bitten through, and a large, open sore on his front leg was bleeding around the edges.

"Hey," I said softly, reaching two fingers through the wooden slats and wiggling them in the dog's direction. "Hey, boy. Hey there."

The dog lunged when he saw me, barking so rapidly that saliva flew out of his mouth. The chain around his neck was just short enough that he couldn't reach the fence or my fingers, but he strained so hard against it that I thought he might choke. At least half of his left ear was missing, as if something had bitten it off, and a thick, gooey fluid leaked out of the corners of his eyes. "Oh, buddy," I whispered. "Who did—"

Something heavy slammed against the fence, nar-rowly missing my fingers. I jumped back so quickly that I fell over.

"Get out of there!" a man's voice growled. "You go on home and mind your business!"

The dog shrank back along the fence and yipped, a high-pitched, terrifying sound that frightened me even more than the voice did. I scrambled to my feet, looking around frantically, but there was no telling where it had come from.

"I said beat it!" I looked up as the voice snarled from above. Leaning out of the second-floor window of the house next door was an old man dressed in a red-and-blue flannel shirt. His gray beard was shaggy and unkempt, and a shotgun with a long silver barrel on one end rested against his left arm. He glared down at me and nudged the gun with his opposite hand. "*Now!*"

I stumbled as I tried to get back up, and fell down again, cutting my hand on a rock. But the only thing I could feel was the bite of the wind against my face and my heart knocking inside my chest as I raced over to the house and burst through Margery's front door.

CHAPTER 2

"Winifred?" Margery's voice floated from somewhere in the back of the house. "That you?"

"Yeah." I leaned over, planting my hands on my knees as I tried to slow my breathing. The edge of my right hand stung, and I winced as I caught sight of the blood trickling down one side.

Margery appeared, wiping her hands on a dish towel. She stopped when she saw the blood and then moved toward me quickly. Tossing the dishcloth over one shoulder, she took my hand in hers, examining the wound. "What happened?"

"I fell."

"Where?"

"Outside."

Margery gave me a look as she turned my hand over. "*Where* outside, Winifred?"

"It's Fred," I said, pulling my hand back. "I like to be called Fred."

"Right." She nodded. "Where did you fall, Fred?"

"By the back fence."

Her face darkened. "You didn't go *over* the fence, did you?"

I shook my head. "Just next to it. By one of the holes. I wanted to see if I could get the dog to stop barking. And then some guy yelled at me to beat it." I paused, not sure if I should mention the gun. "So I ran. And then I tripped."

She looked at me silently for a moment and then balled the dish towel under my hand. "Come on in the kitchen. I have iodine and bandages to wrap this up."

I followed her down a short hallway, holding the towel with my other hand. The floors in the house were hardwood, bare for the most part, except for one or two small rugs. At the end of the hallway was the kitchen. It was enormous, maybe even the entire length of the house, and half as wide. The walls had been painted a bright yellow, and a real fireplace sat at one end, big and broad as two ovens. Flames sparked and crackled atop five or six logs, and the scent of woodsmoke filled the room. It was warm and cozy.

"Have a seat." Margery pulled a chair out from under a long table and walked over to a row of cupboards. I sat down. The chair was metal with a tall, solid back. I turned, peering carefully at the back of it, startled to realize that what I'd thought were scribbles were, in fact, carefully etched designs. There were leaves and vines, flowers and branches and crescent moons, even a tiny mouse with whiskers peeking out from one of the corners. I stared at the mouse, examining the small ears and the hint of a tail, which disappeared around the edge.

"You find the fox in there?" Margery pulled out a chair next to me and sat down, plunking a brown bottle, a white box, and a little silver bowl onto the table. "He's a tough one. You've got to look real hard."

I turned around, embarrassed that she'd caught me looking at all. I hoped she couldn't tell I was impressed, either. Stuff like that just led to trouble.

"Hold your hand out over this bowl," she directed.

I did as she said, sucking in hard as she poured the brown liquid over the cut.

"You like dogs, Fred?" Margery blotted my hand again and placed a square of cotton over the top of it.

"I guess."

"You ever have one?"

"No." I'd wanted a dog for as long as I could remember, but Mom said they were too much work. She had a hard enough time trying to take care of the two of us, she always said. A dog would make things impossible.

"Well, let me tell you something about that dog next door." Margery ripped a piece of surgical tape with her teeth and placed it over one side of the bandage. "He belongs to John Carder. And John Carder is probably the meanest person on God's green earth."

I thought about the horrible chain biting into the dog's neck, the gooey stuff leaking from his eyes, and the ear that looked like it had been bitten off. I wasn't about to argue.

Margery nodded as she finished taping the other side of the bandage. "If you're here long enough, you'll find out that Mr. Carder never brings him inside, either. Rain or snow, ice or wind, that poor animal is attached to his pole."

My mouth dropped open. "Even during the winter?"

"Twenty-four/seven." Margery's voice was grim. "Although he does have a little shed now. Carder built it last year after the ASPCA called and threatened to take the dog. There might be a ratty old blanket in there. Maybe a bone. But the dog never goes inside Mr. Carder's house. And in all the years I've lived here, I've never seen the man give that animal a pat on the head or say a kind word to him."

"And you're okay with this?"

"Of course I'm not okay with it." Margery got up and put the supplies back in the cupboard. She filled a copper teakettle with water and put it on the stove to boil. "Who do you think called the ASPCA?"

"You?"

"You bet. And before that, I went over and tried to talk some sense into the man. I even offered to take the dog myself."

"But he wouldn't listen?"

"Oh, he listened," she said. "And then he told me that if I ever came on his property again, he'd shoot me right between the eyes. I'm only going to tell you this once, Fred. I know you feel sorry for that animal. And he will probably keep trying to get your attention by barking on and on the way he does. But you cannot, no matter what, go anywhere near him or the Carder place." She paused, studying me. "Promise me."

I could feel something flare inside me. I'd known this lady for all of three, maybe four hours, and she was already ordering me around? Making me *promise* things? "You're not my mother," I said. "And I wouldn't go near that disgusting dog anyway, even if you paid me."

Margery held my gaze for a moment. Her eyes were the color of cornflowers. "Well, I guess we're okay, then."

"Yeah," I said. "I guess we are."

She turned around as the kettle began to whistle. "You drink tea?"

"No."

"How about a hot bath? You can soak for as long as you want while I finish dinner, and then we can eat here by the fire."

"A bath?" I could feel my face flush. Did I *look* like I needed a bath? Or worse, did I stink? The water at our apartment back home had been turned off for almost four days, but I'd been washing off every morning in the locker room at school. Maybe I hadn't been doing a good enough job.

"I've got a great tub upstairs," Margery said. "You'll love it. Come on."

I followed her up a flight of stairs and into a bathroom, which was about the size of Mom's and my entire apartment. The walls were a pale blue color, and a window on the opposite end had been hung with green-and-white-checkered curtains.

"You ever taken a soak in a nineteenth-century claw-foot bathtub?" Margery asked.

"Nope." I couldn't remember the last time I'd taken a soak at all. Our bathtub at home was too short to stretch my legs out straight, and no matter how much I scrubbed, the rusty orange ring around the drain never went away.

"Well, then, today's your lucky day." Margery went over to the tub and turned the faucet on. She reached into a cupboard and pulled out a thick yellow towel, a wash-cloth, and a small bottle with a rubber stopper. "This here's lavender bubble bath. It's my favorite, so don't go crazy. You just need a few drops. This stuff bubbles up like some kind of science experiment."

I took the bottle from her gingerly, wondering if it was some kind of trick. This lady, who was as tall and broad as a man, and rode a motorcycle named Luke Jackson, took bubble baths?

"Here's shampoo and conditioner, too." Margery placed two bottles next to the tub. "Don't be afraid to use a little on that head of yours after you're done soaking." She looked around. "Is that everything?"

"I need my clothes," I said. "You know, the ones that Carmella gave me back at the office? In the paper bag?"

"Oh." Margery frowned. "Right. They're still in the wash."

"The wash?"

She shrugged. "They were a little grungy-looking. I went through them when you were outside. I was going to put them in your dresser drawers, but then I changed my mind and decided to wash them first. I should have asked you, though. I apologize."

"It's okay." I could feel my cheeks getting hot again and I tried to push down my annoyance. It was bad enough that I'd had to take hand-me-downs from some closet at the Children and Youth Services building because there hadn't been time for me to go home and pack, but now I had to deal with Margery deciding to do whatever she wanted with them. Where was my say in any of this? Why did adults always just assume that they knew better? "It's just . . . I don't have anything else."

"Hold on a second." I stood there, watching the tub fill as Margery swept past me. I could see the dog from the bathroom window. He'd settled down finally and was lying in the dirt, licking the wound on his leg.

Margery reappeared, a gigantic purple fuzzy bathrobe draped over one arm. "It's mine," she said, hanging it on a hook inside the door. "So it'll be a little big. But just pull it tight and double-knot the belt so it won't fall off. You can wear it until your clothes are done."

Two barks sounded outside the window, but without the frantic edge from before. Now they just sounded lonely. And tired.

"Does that dog even have a name?" I asked.

"Toby, I think." Margery gave me a look that said the topic was closed.

And before I could say another word, she walked out of the bathroom and shut the door.

CHAPTER 3

I got the worst part over first, washing my hair twice and then dumping on a big blob of conditioner. I ran my fingers through it, loosening all the knots, and then piled it on top of my head. It smelled like coconut and green grass, and I leaned back, resting my arms along the bath's ceramic edge. The tub was big enough that even with my legs stretched all the way out, there was still room left over. It was so clean that the sides of it gleamed. No rust. No mildew. The woodsy scent of the lavender bubble bath hung in the air, and the late-afternoon light filtered through the curtains. It was like heaven, being in there. Like heaven and then some.

But it didn't last. Especially when I thought about Mom. I knew that the possibility of her enjoying a bath like this was nonexistent. What was she doing just now? What was she thinking?

I drifted back to the day before, trying to connect the dots. What had I missed? Was there anything that might have hinted at all the trouble that had unfolded today? Mom had been a little antsy last night, but that wasn't anything new. She was always a little irritable after work, mostly because her boss at the pharmacy, a short, mean man named Mr. McCormick, made her do jobs that no one else wanted to do, like stock the laxative shelves and dust the walls behind the soda machines, where gigantic, floaty cobwebs lived. She was always tired at the end of her shift. Tired and worn-out and sometimes even a little bit teary.

Last night, though, she was just edgy. I was sitting on the couch in the living room, wrapped in my comforter, trying to finish the first chapter of A Wrinkle in Time. It was hard to concentrate because it was so cold in the apartment, and while my body was warm, the tips of my nose and fingers were like ice. Mom had said we'd get the heat turned back on along with the water after she got paid on Friday, but right then, it was hard to think about anything else.

I was just starting chapter two when she came out of the bedroom and wandered into the kitchen. Her hair hung loosely around her shoulders, and she'd pulled on a pair of fuzzy socks, sweatpants, and a T-shirt. I looked up from my book as she started opening and shutting the cupboard doors. I could feel my Mom radar flicking on, my uh-oh antennae snapping to attention. "What do you need?" I called from the couch. "Did you lose something?"

"No, no." She opened the refrigerator and stared inside, her hand on the door. I could see the veins running along the inside of her arm. They stuck out like little green caterpillars from her wrist all the way up to her elbow. She was getting too skinny again.

"Are you hungry?" I dog-eared the page in my book and got up from the couch. "You want me to make you another grilled cheese?"

She closed the refrigerator and looked at me. Her eyes were glassy, and for a minute, I wondered if she'd taken the wrong pill. Mom took lots of pills, the slim orange bottles lined up beside her bed like a row of soldiers. Some of them helped her sleep, others made her relax, and still others gave her a little extra boost when she needed it. It wasn't a big deal, she'd told me; everyone needed something to get through the day, and anyone who said they didn't was lying. She was right, too. My English teacher always had a cup of coffee in her hand. And every morning, when Mom turned the corner to head into work, I knew her friend Gwyneth waited for her outside the Rite Aid, smoking a cigarette. So Mom needed a pill or two. As long as she kept on being Mom, I was okay with that.

"Mom?" I went over and rubbed her arm. "What's wrong?" I nodded toward the pile of blankets in the living room. "You want to get under the covers?" She shook her head and leaned into me. I stroked her hair as she began to cry. "Mom, what is it?" I didn't like it when she cried. It made me nervous.

"I just wish it wasn't like this," she said.

"Like what?" I steered her slowly toward the couch. "Everything's fine."

"No, it's not." Her voice cracked. "We don't have any heat or water, there's hardly any food in the kitchen, and I'm just . . ." She shook her head. "I'm just not cutting it here, Fred. You deserve so much better."

"Shhhh . . ." I tilted her head against my shoulder and rubbed her arm. She got this way sometimes, sinking down in the dumps about everything that was going wrong instead of focusing on the things that were going right. I knew what to do because I'd done it a hundred times. "Everything's fine, Mom. It really is. Let's look at it one step at a time, okay?" I ticked the points off on my fingers. "You're getting paid in a few days, which means we'll have heat again. And water. We had grilled cheeses for dinner, which"—I nudged her in the side—"were pretty darn good, if I do say so myself. Even if I did burn the back of mine. And we have each other."

Mom took my hand in hers. "We do, don't we?" she murmured.

"We do." I nodded, running my fingertips up and down the top of her hand. "Which is more important than all the rest of it anyway."

"You're right." She took a deep breath and then let it out again. "Oh, Fred, what would I do without you?"

"You don't have to worry about that," I said, squeezing her hand. "Because we'll never have to find out."

Until we did.

Today.

One minute I was in Mr. Poole's third-period science class, and the next minute I was sitting in an office at Children and Youth Services, waiting for Carmella to tell me what had happened to Mom. For some reason, it hadn't hit me yet how serious everything was; I actually thought I was going to be able to go back to school, and maybe even squeak my way into the last round of Science Jeopardy, for which I'd been studying for weeks. Right up until everything happened, Science Jeopardy was kind of the most exciting thing going on in my life. Mostly because I was good at science. And because I knew I could win Science Jeopardy, which Mr. Poole held at the start of every new marking period.

Carmella had a poster on her wall that said LIFE IS TOUGH, BUT SO ARE YOU! in thick, multicolored letters, and a plant with long, snakelike leaves hanging down the front of the desk. It reminded me of one of the questions Mr. Poole had asked during the first round of Science Jeopardy, and the only one—in all four rounds—that I had gotten wrong. The question was, which tissue carries sugary sap around a plant? The answer is phloem, which is pronounced FLO-em, and which I will probably never in this lifetime ever forget again. But at that moment, my brain went totally blank. Now all I could think, staring at those weird plant tendrils on Mrs. Rivers's desk, was the word "phloem." Phloem. Phloem.

That is, until Carmella started typing on her laptop. "Hey," I said. "You were going to tell me where my mom is when we got here. Well, we're here."

Carmella glanced up at me. Her brown hair looked like a Brillo pad, and she had dark, bushy eyebrows. "Right now, she's at the police station," she said quietly.

Something lurched inside my chest. "The *police* station? Why?"

"We're still not sure."

"What do you mean, you're not sure?" I squeezed my fists. "You've gotta know something!"

"We're still waiting to hear the rest of the story. All I know right now, honey, is that there was an incident at Rite Aid."

"Don't call me honey." I spoke through gritted teeth. "And why do you keep using the word 'incident'? What *happened*?"

"We don't know the details yet." She looked at me hopefully as the phone rang. "Hold on. This might give us some more information."

I held my breath as she picked up the phone. "Carmella speaking." She held my eyes as someone spoke to her on the other end, and then nodded, indicating that the person was talking about Mom. "Yes, okay. Go ahead." I held my breath. Bit my lower lip.

After another moment, Carmella dropped her eyes. A muscle pulsed in her jaw as she drew her index finger along the edge of her desk. My heart sank. It wasn't going to be good, whatever it was. I pressed my sneakers to the floor as hard as I could and dug my thumbnail into my palm.

"Okay." Carmella sighed heavily and scribbled something on a yellow pad next to her laptop. "All right. Yes. Okay. Last name again? Uh-huh. Okay, then. Thanks, Sherry."

She put the phone back in the hook and raised her eyes again.

"What?" I asked.

Carmella's voice was somber. "We're not sure what the full extent of charges are yet, but it does look as though your mother is going to jail for a little while."

"*Jail?*" I shot up, as if something from above had yanked me to my feet. "What do you mean, jail?"

"I know you're upset." Carmella held her hands out as if I might lunge across the desk. "But please—"

"Why are they sending her to jail?" My voice was shaking. It was too loud, but I didn't care. "What did she do? What's going to happen?"

"The police found some pills on her. That she'd stolen. From the Rite Aid."

"No, no, no!" I shook my head back and forth. "Those are *her* pills! She always has them! She takes them for anxiety and pain and stuff. They thought she *stole* them? From the store?"

"That's what they're saying."

"Well, they're wrong!" I sat back down. "They're totally, one hundred million percent wrong! My mom would never do something like that. I bet that stupid manager of hers . . ." I stood back up. "I want to go down and talk to them. To any of them. I'll let them know. I'll tell them . . ."

"Oh, honey, it doesn't work that way." Carmella shook her head. "You've got to leave it up to them now. They'll sort everything out."

"Sort what out?" I was breathing hard now, my brain racing. "She didn't *do* anything!" For a moment, I wondered if I was dreaming, if I'd wake up suddenly in my bed at the apartment, shaking and breathless, realizing I'd imagined it all. But that didn't happen.

And before I could say anything else, Carmella took my hand. "We have someone coming for you, honey. To take care of you for a while. Her name is Margery Dawson. She's a first-time foster parent, so I think she's just as nervous about the situation as you might be. But she's a wonderful woman. She lives in Lancaster, which is about eighty miles from here, so it'll be a big change from the city, and she . . ."

She went on and on, but I'd stopped listening.

I wasn't even sure I was still breathing.

Just like that, my life had turned upside down and

inside out. And now here I was, soaking in a forty-gallon bathtub while Mom was sitting in a jail cell all by herself.

I slid under the water, holding my breath and squeezing my eyes shut.

It was the only thing I could do to keep the tears from coming.

CHAPTER 4

"Not bad." Margery flicked her eyes at me as I appeared in the kitchen, dressed in her robe. She was taking a tin of muffins out of the oven. They were a golden-yellow color, with slightly brown tops. "It fits you better than I would've thought."

I shoved the sleeves up along my arms and sat down. I wasn't sure what kind of eyesight Margery had, but I was drowning in her dumb robe. The hem dragged on the floor, and I'd had to wrap the belt twice around my waist just to keep it up. Still, it was soft. And even though my hair was wet and dripped down my back, I was warm and dry.

Margery set a plate and the muffin tin down on the table in front of me. She held up a butter knife and tossed another dish towel over one shoulder. "Watch me first." She ran the knife around the edges of one of the muffins and then slid it out. "Just like that, okay?" She put the muffin on the plate and handed me the knife. "Think you can do it?"

I nodded and stood, shoving up the sleeves of the robe. It was harder than it looked. The first two muffins split and broke in half as I tried to take them out of the tin, and the third one only came halfway out. I did okay with the rest of them, and I shoved the broken ones in the middle of the platter, squishing them in tight so that Margery wouldn't notice. They were the size of baseballs, and they smelled a little like Rice Krispies Treats.

Margery glanced over at the finished plate and nodded. "Nice work. You mind setting the table now?" She opened a cupboard above the counter. "The dishes are up there. We're having beef stew, so we need big bowls. And maybe a few of the smaller plates for the corn muffins. There's napkins in the drawer and a salt-and-pepper set above it."

I set everything out slowly, marveling at the beautiful cream-colored plates with scalloped edges, the heavy silverware, and the cloth napkins. Mom and I mostly just ate off paper plates. Sometimes we had squares of paper towel for napkins, but if I'd forgotten to buy it, we didn't use anything at all.

"All right!" Margery brought over a deep-blue bowl filled with chunks of beef and carrot and potato. She ladled it into my bowl, adding extra gravy and carrots on top, and then filled her own. "Beef stew is one of my favorites." She sat down and spread a napkin on her lap. "I hope you like it."

I didn't realize how hungry I was until I took the first bite. Then I wasn't sure I'd be able to stop. I ended up wolfing down two and half bowls of the stew and two corn muffins as Margery watched. Every so often she would nod or smile, but she didn't say anything and neither did I. Behind us, the fire spit and crackled, and when I finally sat back and took a long, deep breath, I realized it might have been the first one I'd taken all day.

After her second corn muffin, Margery sat back in her chair, too. She wiped her mouth and placed her napkin on the table next to her plate. "So. How're you doing, Fred?"

I turned my head and glared at her.

"I mean . . ." Margery gestured with her hands. "You know, all things considered."

I shrugged. What did she expect me to say? That things were great? That my mother was in jail and I didn't know when she'd get out, let alone when I'd see her again, but now that I had taken a bath and eaten a bowl of beef stew, everything was just fine and dandy?

Margery cleared her throat. She took a sip from her tea and placed the mug back down, wrapping her hands around the outside of it. "I guess that was a dumb question." She inhaled deeply and blew it back out. "Let me start over. Are you tired?"

I shook my head, but that wasn't true. I was exhausted. And yet, I didn't know if I'd ever be able to sleep again.

Margery nodded, as if she'd expected me to say no. "We should probably talk about a curfew, then."

I looked up. "I'm not going anywhere."

"I know." Margery shrugged. "But you know, for lights-out. Bedtime and all that. What do you do at home? What time do you go to sleep?"

I shrugged. "Whenever."

"You don't have a curfew?"

"Not really." Mom was usually asleep for hours before I crawled into bed, and I just fell asleep when I was tired, not when the numbers on a clock said it was time to close my eyes.

"Okay, well, maybe while you're here, we'll agree on a bedtime." Margery threaded a long braid of hair through her fingers as she spoke. "Especially on school nights. How about nine o'clock?"

I rolled my eyes. "I'm twelve years old, not five."

"Nine thirty?"

"Ten thirty."

Margery shook her head. "Too late. You'll have to be up by six every morning to catch the bus here. How about ten?"

I was up at six every morning back home, no matter what time I fell asleep, not because I wanted to, or even because I needed to, but because that was when Mom got up. She tried to be quiet, but the fold-up bed across the room always squeaked when she doubled it back up, and whenever I heard it, my eyes flew open. She would tiptoe over and kiss me on the forehead and tell me to go back to sleep, but I never did. I'd just lie there and listen as she moved around the apartment, making coffee, brushing her teeth, opening and closing the kitchen cupboards. It was odd, I guess, but hearing those little noises always made me feel as though everything was okay. It was when the sounds stopped that I worried.

"Fine," I muttered. "Ten."

"Good." Margery nodded. "That wasn't too bad. How about breakfast? Is there anything you won't eat? Can't eat? Eggs, maybe?"

"I hardly ever eat in the morning."

"How come?"

I shrugged. "Not hungry."

Margery paused, and for a split second, I thought she could tell I was lying. I braced myself for another back-and-forth, but it didn't come. "How about if you were?" she asked instead. "What if you woke up tomorrow morning and you were absolutely starving? What would you want to eat if you could eat anything?"

It was a huge question. My brain whirled, trying to imagine the possibilities, but I couldn't get past stale Frosted Flakes, which was all we ever had at home. "No idea," I said, poking the side of my bowl with my spoon.

"Oatmeal?" Margery encouraged.

I shrugged.

"Waffles?"

"Sure."

"How about an everything bagel with cream cheese, sliced tomato, and a hard-fried egg on top?"

I looked up. "What's an everything bagel?"

Margery's eyes went wide and then softened again. "You'll find out in the morning." She tossed her braid back over one shoulder and reached for my bowl. "Finished?" I nodded. She took the bowl and put it inside of hers. Then she stood up. "I'm going to put these in the dishwasher and pull your clothes out of the dryer. They should be just about done."

"Okay." I could feel her eyes on me as I lifted up her robe and headed toward the stairs.

"Your bedroom is the first one on the left," she called. "I'll be up in a few minutes."

I kept walking.

"Oh, and, Fred?"

I stopped and looked down at the floor.

"If you can think of anything else you might need, don't hesitate to ask."

Man, I wished she'd stop being so nice. It wasn't that I wanted her to be mean or anything; it was just that her obvious concern for me made me like her a little bit. And I didn't want to like her. I didn't want to *dislike* her. I just didn't want to feel anything toward her. Not feeling anything was easiest.

I made my way upstairs, where I sat on the edge of the bed. I was exhausted, but I didn't want to go to sleep. Mostly because I didn't want morning to come. If it was any other morning, I'd get dressed for school and Mom would get dressed for work, and we'd walk the first three blocks together, holding hands and singing Lady Gaga songs until we reached Woodrow Wilson Middle School. Right before I went inside, Mom would take my face in her hands and tilt it up a little.

"I love you," she'd say.

"I love you, too."

She'd start to grin. "I love you three."

"I love you four."

She'd grab me in a hug. "I love you more." She would kiss the tip of my nose and stand there at the end of the sidewalk until I disappeared inside the front doors.

Neither of us would be able to do that tomorrow. And I couldn't be sure when we ever would again.

CHAPTER 5

There was a skylight above my bed, and for a long time that evening, I just stared up at the inky rectangle of black, trying to make out a few stars that glittered in the left-hand corner. Last year, my sixth-grade science teacher had taught us that some stars, which scientists called binary stars, came in pairs. When I told Mom about it later that night, she kissed me and said that was what we were—two shiny binary stars, drifting in the heavens.

My belly was full and I was clean and warm and comfortable beneath Margery's flannel sheets, but remembering that made me so sad just then that it literally hurt to take a breath. Every time I inhaled, something inside would catch and then crack a little, and the more I thought about it, the bigger the cracks got, until I thought that maybe something really had broken inside.

And then I heard it.

A long, terrible howl outside my window. I held my

breath as it dipped and then faded, a small, mournful cornucopia of sound. A few seconds later, it came again, longer and even more despondent than the first one, and this time I got out of bed. I tiptoed across the room and pushed the curtains to one side so that I could look over at Mr. Carder's yard. Toby was sitting on his haunches with his head tipped back, wailing so pitifully that it made my teeth hurt. I pressed my hand against the cold glass and listened to my heart thump inside my chest. I knew that if I could push what I was feeling out of my chest just then, it would have sounded exactly like that howl.

"Shut your trap!" Mr. Carder's voice shot out from the upstairs window. It was followed by a heavy thud.

Toby yelped as something hit the ground a few inches away from him. He ducked behind his tattered shed and stayed there for a moment without moving. I could only make out the barest outline of him since it was so dark, but I watched as he licked his haunches and then slowly, slowly settled himself down on the ground, resting his head between his front paws. He looked defeated. Exhausted.

And utterly alone.

I grabbed the comforter off my bed and snatched the smaller blanket beneath it. It was late—the digital clock next to my bed read 1:06 a.m.—but I didn't care. I rummaged through the dresser drawers, pulled on two long-sleeve T-shirts, a pair of jeans, and a hoodie, and tiptoed down to the kitchen.

Inside the refrigerator was a blue-and-yellow ceramic bowl covered with plastic wrap. I grabbed it and looked inside. Bingo! Tucking the bowl into the crook of my arm, I snuck out a side door and closed it softly behind me.

As I looked out at the darkness with my arms full of blankets and beef stew, for a split second I thought of turning around and going back in again. I'd been outside at night lots of times of course, but it was different in the city. The streetlights were always on, and even at one in the morning, someone was always awake, driving down McCord Avenue or walking along the sidewalk.

The darkness here wasn't like any darkness I'd ever seen before. It was total. Complete. Like being covered with a blanket or walking into a cave and having the opening sealed shut. There was a sliver of a moon overhead, and even though I knew that the moon was the second-brightest object in the sky after the sun, it didn't feel very bright. And it sure wasn't giving off much light.

I could feel the hairs on my arms stand up and the pounding of my heart inside my chest. And then I heard the clink of the chain in Mr. Carder's yard. The soft movement as Toby shifted his weight in the dirt, followed by a long, doleful sigh.

I took a deep breath and started walking.

Woof! Woof!
"Hush your mouth!"

"Fred! Can you hear me?"

I thought I was dreaming at first, all those noises and voices, coming from somewhere far away. Big hands shook me awake, and all at once, like a slap, I felt the cold. The sun was out, shining directly above me, but I couldn't feel my cheeks or the tip of my nose. Even my bones felt cold, all the way to the inside and then back out again. I shivered and burrowed down more tightly into the comforter around me.

"Fred!" It was Margery. "Fred, you have to get up. Come on. Right now."

Woof!

"I want to know what in tarnation is going on," uttered a growly voice. "And if I don't get an answer, we're going to have some serious issues!"

"Don't you threaten me, John." There was an edge to Margery's voice that I hadn't heard yet. "She's not on your property. Besides, we're leaving."

"She's fooling with my dog!" the old man spat back. "And my dog is my property!"

Woof!

I got to my feet slowly, my body stiff and sore. My neck felt lopsided, as if I had lain on it wrong, and my toes were asleep. I wrapped the comforter around me more tightly and looked over at Toby. He was straining against his chain, the tip of his nose barely reaching the small opening where we'd lain, side by side, all night. I'd been able to wedge the bowl of beef stew through when he'd first caught sight of me, and after he'd eaten it all, I'd wrenched a little bit more of the rotted section of fence away so that I could stretch my hand through the opening and pat him. He smelled terrible and his fur was matted down to just a little bald spot on the top of his head, but I kept stroking him and telling him what a good boy he was. He licked my hand so hard and for so long that I knew he was trying to tell me something. He wasn't just grateful for the food. He was grateful I was there. He was afraid I would leave again. More than anything in the world, he just wanted me to stay.

And so I stretched out the comforter next to the broken slat of fence and rolled myself up in it, and when Toby lay down on his side of the yard, I reached in and draped the other, smaller blanket over him. His eyes were so sad and so grateful, and even though it was cold, I slid my hand through the little fence slat again so that he could lick it. He licked it and licked it and licked it, and that was the last thing I remembered before I fell asleep.

"She's not fooling with anything," Margery said now in the same stiff voice she'd used before. "It looks like she just came out here to give the poor animal some company, and she fell asleep." She turned, looking at me. Her face was flushed and her jaw was set like a square. I couldn't tell if she was angry with Mr. Carder or me. "Is that right, Fred? Is that what happened?"

Woof!

I nodded.

Mr. Carder grunted as he leaned down to retrieve something. "Just comp'ny, huh? Then what do you call this?"

Margery and I both ducked as he hurled the bowl over the fence. I stared wide-eyed as it landed heavily in Margery's yard, rolled a little bit, and then settled upside down among the leaves like a large blue-and-yellow mushroom cap.

"Is that my bowl?" Margery seemed less concerned with the fact that Mr. Carder had thrown her dish than she was with it being outside. "Fred, is that my bowl? Did you bring my bowl out here?"

"Yeah." I cleared my throat. "I kind of figured he'd be hungry."

"That was . . ." Margery narrowed her eyebrows. "That was the rest of the stew." It was a statement, not a question.

I nodded.

"You have no right goin' and feedin' my animal!" Mr. Carder's eyes were hard little slits. "He gets what I give him, and that's plenty. It's more'n enough." He stuck a gnarled finger in my direction. "You stay away from my dog." He jabbed his finger in the air. "He's mine, you hear? *Mine!*"

Toby was watching me, waiting, I could tell, for me to turn around and walk away from him. His eyes were heavy, like he was bracing himself for my turned back, getting ready for me to disappear behind a closed door.

Maybe I'd made a mistake, coming out here and showing him some affection. Maybe giving such a thing, only to have it taken away again, was worse than never having it at all.

"There's no need to yell, Mr. Carder." Margery tugged on one end of the comforter. "I'm sure she's heard you loud and clear."

"She better have." Mr. Carder spun on the heel of his boot. " 'Specially if she knows what's good for her." He stomped up his front steps and disappeared behind a slammed door.

"Let's go." Margery strode across the lawn, stooped down to pick up her bowl, and headed for the house. "Now, Fred!" Her voice was sharp.

I kept Toby's gaze level with mine as I dropped my voice to a whisper. "Don't you worry, okay? I'll come back to see you as soon as I can. I promise." I moved across the lawn slowly, one backward step at a time. Toby's pink nose quivered as the distance between us increased, and then, just as I reached the front door, I held up my hand, a short little wave, before I disappeared inside again.

Woof!

CHAPTER 6

"Come in here and sit down, please." I stopped in my tracks as Margery called from the kitchen. There was no mistaking the tone of her voice.

"I'm going to get dressed fir—"

"You are going to get in this kitchen." Margery appeared in the hallway, pointing behind her. "Now."

I plunked down in one of the chairs, clutching the comforter around my shoulders.

Margery sat down across from me and rested her hands on the table. Man, they were big. Like paws. I hunkered down inside the comforter a little bit more and held my breath.

"Do you remember what I told you yesterday about that dog?"

I looked down at the table.

"I made you promise me—"

"I didn't promise you anything." I lifted my head. "I didn't."

"That's right," Margery said. "You didn't have to. Because you said you wouldn't go near that disgusting dog even if someone paid you."

"I changed my mind."

"He's not yours."

"He shouldn't be Mr. Carder's."

Margery shook her head. "But he is, Fred. And I know it's awful that someone can treat an animal like that and get away with it, but there's nothing we can do about it."

I didn't want to get on this merry-go-round again. There weren't any answers. Or at least, none that made any sense. Instead, I pressed my lips together and stared down at the table, which was bare, now that last night's tablecloth had been taken off. It was mostly metal and fashioned somehow out of five or six gigantic wheels, all stuck together side by side. A large plate of glass covered the wheels so that there was a stable, flat surface to eat on, but the rest of it was just the wheels and a strange mishmash of metal parts.

"Did you make this table?" I pointed down at the wheels.

Margery sat back in her seat, looking slightly confused. "Yes."

"How?"

She shrugged. "I found the wheels and cleaned them up and made them into a table."

"Where'd you find them?"

"Just sitting in front of someone's house, I think. Big 'For Free' sign on the front of them."

"You take people's junk?"

"Sometimes. Only things that I think really have potential. Things I know I can make something out of."

"How do you know?"

Margery shrugged. "It's kind of a feeling, I guess." She glanced over as the copper teakettle began to whistle. "You learn as you go." She got up, flicked off the flame, and poured boiling water into two mugs.

"I told you I don't drink—"

"It's not tea," Margery said. "It's Mexican hot chocolate." She shook a tiny tin over the mugs. "You need to drink something hot to warm up those bones of yours. They must be practically frostbitten after lying on the ground all night." She raised an eyebrow in my direction. "It's October, Fred. Not July."

"What's Mexican hot chocolate?" I asked, sidestepping her comment.

"Have you ever had regular hot chocolate?" Margery placed the mugs on the table.

"Sure." I leaned over and peered into mine. A thick, creamy foam, sprinkled with something that looked like brown freckles blanketing the top of it. "But nothing that looks like this."

"That's because it's made with very, very good dark chocolate, ground-up chipotle peppers, and cinnamon."

Margery took a sip from her mug and closed her eyes. "Go on and give it a try. It'll warm you right up."

"There's *peppers* in it?" I drew back in disgust.

"Try it before you snub it."

I lifted the mug to my mouth. The scent of cinnamon was okay, but there was something else, something biting and harsh-smelling that made me wrinkle my nose. "I don't think so."

"Just a sip." Margery took another gulp of hers and raised an eyebrow. "I dare you."

I brought the mug to my lips again and took a tiny sip. The warmth of the liquid felt so good sliding down my throat that I shuddered. But a few seconds later, a different heat filled my mouth. It was spicy and a little tingly, but delicious, too, in an odd, almost unsettling way. "Wow," I breathed, taking another sip. "That's really good."

"I told you." Margery leaned forward. "I know what I'm talking about. Especially when it comes to food, junk, and neighbors." She waited until I looked at her. "You've *got* to stay away from that dog, Fred. If you don't, I'll have to call Carmella and tell her that it just won't work out."

My eyes narrowed. "You'd do that?"

"I wouldn't want to." Margery paused. "But I won't be able to live with myself if that man goes off and does something foolish because you've decided to feed his dog again." She leaned in a little closer. "When I tell you that

John Carder is the world's meanest person, I'm not exaggerating. He's miserable and rotten and full of hate and I don't know why he's that way, but it doesn't matter. What does matter is that he's capable of anything, and he's got nothing to lose, which makes him even more dangerous."

Margery's nostrils were white around the edges, and there was a little bit of spit in the corner of her mouth. I'd only needed the past twenty-four hours to learn that she was a tough cookie. Maybe one of the toughest I'd ever met. But she had a nice side, too. She was fair. And generous. And a pretty good cook. I didn't want to go back to Carmella's office and wait for her to find me some other strange family that might be willing to take me. It was too much of a risk. Too much more to lose.

"Okay," I said.

"Okay, what?"

"Okay, I'll stay away from the fence."

"And the dog."

I nodded. "And the dog."

Margery sat back again. Her nostrils softened and the square in her chin went back to its soft, round shape. "Thank you." She stood up. "Now, you ready for your everything bagel?"

I shrugged. "I guess."

Margery reached into a brown paper bag and withdrew a bagel. I recoiled at the sight of all the strange specks that dotted the outside and made a face. "I'm not eating that."

"These are just seeds," Margery said. "Poppy, sesame, caraway. There's salt on it, too, and a little dried garlic and onion. That's why it's called an everything bagel. Because they put a little bit of everything on it. Give it a try, at least."

I didn't say any more. She'd been right about the Mexican hot chocolate. Maybe she was right about this, too. I watched as she sliced the bagel down the middle and dropped it into a toaster.

"Tomorrow's a big day for you," Margery said, taking the cream cheese out of the fridge. "First day at Conestoga Middle School."

"*Tomorrow*?"

"Well, yeah. Tomorrow's Wednesday. You went to school on Wednesdays in Philadelphia, didn't you?"

"Well, yeah, but . . ."

"But what?"

I didn't know what, exactly. It just seemed like too soon. I hadn't even gotten the feel for Margery's place yet. I wasn't ready to dive into another unknown arena. And this one would be with kids my age. Strangers who would stare at me and wonder who I was and where I had come from and what my story was. Then, when they figured out I wasn't going to tell anyone anything, they would make things up and whisper things behind their hands about me. So no, I wasn't ready.

I wasn't ready at all.

CHAPTER 7

The bus picked me up at 6:40 a.m. sharp, just as Margery had said it would. I was the only one at the bus stop, which was at the end of her driveway, and until we stopped again another twenty minutes later, I was the only kid on the bus, too. This was fine with me. Actually, it was more than fine with me. I walked all the way to the back of the bus and sat down in the very last seat. I ate my everything bagel as slowly as I could. Margery had spread it with cream cheese and topped it with two slices of tomato, and it was hard to imagine anything tasting so good.

When I was finished, I wiped my hands on the napkin she had given me and lay down flat on the seat. I could see out the window as the bus moved. The sky was white as a sheet, and a dark wedge of geese flew high above in a perfect V formation. I remembered Mrs. Rogers telling us in fourth grade that the reason geese flew in a V formation was so they could conserve energy. Every goose in line flew slightly higher than the goose behind it, which reduced the wind resistance on the whole group. I closed my eyes. Tried not to remember the bird from the apartment. But it was impossible.

It had been a hot summer night. So hot, in fact, that Mom opened all the windows. We had curtains, long white ones that reached all the way down to the floor, but no screens. Mom wouldn't be able to get screens until she got her next paycheck.

It must have been close to midnight when I got up to use the bathroom. I turned on the bathroom light, and when I did, a little bird that had been sitting in the sink flew past me, soft as a breath, and out into the hall.

"Mom!" I yelled, running into our room and pushing her awake. "Mom, get up! There's a bird in the house!"

She shot up in bed as if the fire alarm had just gone off. "What? Who? What?"

"A bird!" I tugged on the sleeve of her T-shirt. "It's in the bathroom! It must have flown in through the window! It's in here! In the apartment! Right now!"

"A bird?" Her face fell. "Oh, Fred, come on." She dropped back down against the mattress and pulled a pillow over her head.

"Mom!" I yanked at the pillow, desperate to get her up. "Mom, I'm not kidding! Come on. You've got to help me."

"Fred, please just let me sleep."

"But there's a *bird* in the house!"

"Then catch it and throw it back outside." Her voice was muffled beneath the pillow.

"I don't know how!"

There was no answer. For a minute, I thought she'd fallen back asleep. Then, "Throw a blanket over it, take it to the window, and shake it out."

"Aren't you going to help me?"

"I'm too tired," she answered. "I can't even think straight right now. You can do it, Fred. Just go. Please, honey."

And so I snuck back down the hall, grabbing the old brown-and-yellow afghan from the living room couch. I could do this. I could. Mom had spent the day cleaning out the ladies' room after the pharmacy's toilet backed up. She needed to rest.

I tiptoed through the living room, turning on lights as I went, in hopes of attracting the bird. But there was no sign of it. I went back to the bathroom and held my breath as I flung the door open. Nothing. The only other room to check was the kitchen.

When I peeked inside, there, sitting directly on top of the sugar canister, was a little brown bird. It was no bigger than a tennis ball, and its beak was a bright yellow color. I held my breath as it caught sight of me, expecting it to fly away, but it only cocked its head.

"Hi there," I said softly.

At the sound of my voice, the bird tilted its head in the opposite direction. Its beady eyes were bright, and even from where I stood, I could see little tips of white on the edges of its feathers.

"Where'd you come from?" I whispered. "Hmmm?"

The bird ruffled its feathers but kept its head very still, watching me.

"You're so sweet," I whispered. "But you can't stay here. You have to go back outside." The afghan in my hands was heavy. If I threw it over the sugar canister, the bird might suffocate before I had a chance to get it outside.

"Here's what I'm going to do." I kept my voice very soft as I took a step backward. "I'm going to go over to that window over there and push the curtains open real wide. That way, you can just fly away. All by yourself. Okay? You think you can do that?"

I dropped the blanket to the floor as I walked backward to the window. The bird watched me, staring from its perch on the sugar canister. I turned around when I got to the window and slid the curtains open. The bird fluttered its feathers a bit at the movement and peered out the window. "See?" I pointed. "That's where you need to go. Outside where you can fly and be free. There's nothing in here for you." I slid down the small wall of cabinets and tucked my knees under my chin. "Go ahead," I whispered. "Fly away now."

I sat there on the afghan, staring at it for what felt like hours, but the bird didn't move. The faint sounds of traffic drifted through the window. A car horn blared and someone yelled an ugly word. But the bird stayed put. My eyes got heavier and heavier, and the next thing I knew, I was squinting against the glare of sunlight as it streamed through the window. I sat up quickly when I remembered, and looked over at the sugar canister on the countertop.

The little bird was still there.

"Good morning." I smiled as it cocked its head. My voice was soft and groggy. "You stayed here all night? Right here with me?"

The bird ruffled its feathers. And then, before I had a chance to say another word, it flew out the window and disappeared.

Now, lying on the seat in the bus, I wondered again about that bird. It must have seen the open window across the room. It must have felt the breeze floating in, beckoning it back outside. So why had it taken it so long to go? Why had it waited there all night with me instead?

I sat up and stared out the window of the bus. Maybe it had been frightened. Of both leaving and staying. Maybe flying out that window had felt like too big a thing just then, especially at night, with only the stars overhead to light the way. Maybe staying had felt difficult, too, as it struggled to make sense of its strange surroundings. Maybe all it had really needed was that long expanse of night to sit there with me and wait for its tiny heart to slow down before gathering its courage and disappearing into the day beyond.

CHAPTER 8

The rest of the day was a blur.

I only remember art class and a girl everyone called Lardvark. Oh, and the principal's office, where I had to sit for two and a half hours, after I got into a fight. In art class. Over the girl everyone called Lardvark.

We didn't have art in my old school; something about money and budget cuts and all that junk. So nothing prepared me for what I saw when I stepped foot into the classroom. It kind of mesmerized me with the sun streaming through its tall glass windows, lighting up papier-mâché airplanes and hot-air balloons and blue and pink and orange birds and butterflies, all dangling from the ceiling on whisper-thin threads. Man, it was nice.

I was just sort of standing there, looking at all of it, when someone shoved me. Or rather, someone shoved Lardvark, who fell into me. My books flew out of my hands, and I staggered forward, just catching myself on the edge of a large granite table. "Hey!"

"Watch out, Lardvark!" a shrill voice spat. "You don't want to crush the new girl, do you?"

The biggest, tallest seventh grader I'd ever seen shrugged her shoulders and stared down at the floor. Her wide face was flushed, and beads of sweat had broken out along her forehead like small pearls. "Holy cannoli!" She coughed nervously, brushing her blond bangs out of her face. "Are you okay? You're not hurt, are you?"

"No, I'm fine." I watched the girl behind Lardvark, the one who had shoved her, as she made her way over to the other side of the table. Her name was Michelle, and I'd noticed her in my homeroom, mostly because when she laughed—which she seemed to do every few minutes—she shrieked. It was a loud, awful sound, something a hyena might make, and I had turned, wondering where it had come from.

Now Michelle glared at me. She had long, very dark hair and dangly earrings with blue stones at the tips. Her sweater, which stopped right at her belly button, was at least three sizes too small for her, and I could see the outline of a phone inside the front pocket of her jeans. "What're *you* looking at?"

"Nothing," I said.

"Then stop staring." She tossed her head and sat down amid a flurry of giggles from two other girls.

Lardvark pulled on my sleeve. "You know that was an accident, right? That I didn't mean to do that? It was a total accident. Really. I just wasn't watching where I was going and . . ."

"Yes, you were," I said. "I saw what happened. She pushed you."

Michelle the hyena girl was talking to her friends, but she stopped midsentence when she realized what I'd said. She stood up, narrowing her eyes at me. "*What'd* you say?" Her head was dangerously cocked; I could tell she was ready for a fight. Behind me, I could feel Lardvark's fingers as they yanked on my T-shirt. I took a step away from her.

"I said you pushed her. Which you did. Everyone saw it."

"Oh, really?" Michelle pretended to act surprised. "Everyone saw it, huh?" She turned to her friend on the right, who was picking at her fingernails and blowing a purple gum bubble. "Sophia, did you see me push Lardvark?"

"Uh-uh," Sophia answered, popping her gum bubble loudly. "I can't imagine you pushing anyone, Michelle."

"How about you, Renee?" Michelle glanced at her other buddy, who was texting furiously on her phone. "Renee!"

Renee looked up, startled. "What?"

"I said, did you see me push Lardvark here on our way in?"

"No!" Renee acted all horrified. "No, you'd never do something like that."

Michelle shrugged and put her hands on her hips. "That's two against one. Whaddya say now?"

Before I had a chance to answer, a small woman, barely taller than me, emerged from a closet on the other side of the room. "All right, everyone," she said, clapping her hands, "it's time to sit down now and stop talking so I can take roll." She perched on a stool and glanced at a piece of paper. "Terry Anderson?" She went down the line of students. "Georgia Granger? Ardelia Lark?"

Lardvark, who had taken a seat next to me, raised her hand as the last name was called. She watched Michelle and me nervously, her eyes flicking back and forth between us like a Ping-Pong ball. Michelle was watching me, too, still waiting for me to acknowledge her last question.

"You pushed her," I hissed, leaning a little across the granite table. "And I don't care what you or your friends say—you and I both know you did."

"Michelle Palmer?"

Without taking her eyes off me, Michelle raised her hand. "Here." She reached up and twirled a piece of her hair, and I could tell she was debating something inside her head. Every muscle in my body tensed as she looked me up and down, taking me in. Whatever came next, I'd be ready.

"Who cares what you think?" she said suddenly, dismissing me with a wave of her hand. "You're just trash."

And that was it. That was all she said. Three little words that flicked a switch inside me. My body moved with a will of its own, flying straight across the granite table. I grabbed and shook and pulled and yelled, and so did Michelle, until someone pulled me back, hauled me off her, yanked me to my feet, and pushed me out into the coolness of the hallway.

I was able to take two deep breaths before the art teacher appeared. Her green eyes flashed. "Office. *Now.*" Her red flats made a soft peeling sound against the linoleum as she marched me down the hall. She didn't say another word until we reached the office door. Then she turned, her hand on the knob. There was a swipe of blue paint on her face. "You might solve your problems like that where you come from. But that's not how we do things here. Especially in my room."

She left me sitting in a red plastic chair across from a secretary who looked like she was about a hundred years old. Then Mr. Coolidge, the principal, opened the door of his office and told me to come in and tell my side of the story. When I was finished, he gave me a two-day suspension, wrote me up in a file, and called Margery to come get me.

CHAPTER 9

"Your first day?" Margery tossed me my helmet as we made our way over to Luke Jackson in the school parking lot. "Really?"

"I'm sorry."

"I'm sorry, too." She swung a long leg over the seat and settled herself. "I had to take my lunch break early to come get you. Now I'm not going to have any time to eat." She snapped the helmet clasp under her chin. "And you don't want to know me when I get hungry."

I sighed and got on the bike behind her.

"You ready?" she asked.

"Yeah."

Margery kicked the stand up, revved the engine, and roared off down the road. Even with the wind blowing against my face, I could feel my cheeks flush hot as I replayed the fight again in my head.

You're just trash. My insides clenched as I remembered

Michelle's words. The look on her face as she'd spit them at me. Like I was a bug on the floor. A rodent. I'd seen a cashier look at Mom that way once, after she'd handed over her food stamp card. The cashier had taken it gingerly, as if it might be dirty, and slowly, disdainfully, swiped it through the register. She glared at Mom as she gave her change and put our stuff in two paper bags. Like we didn't deserve to eat because we got help from the government. Like we were trash because Mom didn't make enough money to pay all our bills and put food on our table.

I'd seen all that again in Michelle's face as she'd looked me up and down in the art room: disgust, pity, and resentment. That day, staring at the cashier, I'd just felt sad. So sad that I held Mom's hand all the way home, giving it little squeezes whenever we crossed the street. Today, though, that sadness was nowhere to be found. It had been replaced with something bigger. Scarier. Something I didn't recognize.

Something I wasn't sure I wanted to recognize, maybe ever again.

"That's strange." Margery stayed put for a moment after she turned the motorcycle off in the driveway. "Carder's truck is still here."

"Why is that strange?" I got off the bike and unfastened my helmet. The wind was sharp, and it blew my hair around my face. Behind the fence, Toby had already started to bark.

"He works down at the pretzel factory in town." Margery's eyes searched the outside of the house. "I've never seen him home before me on a weekday. Ever."

"Maybe he took a day off."

"Yeah." Margery swung herself off the bike. "Maybe."

Toby continued to bark, more frantically now. I glanced at the bottom of the fence where the hole had been to see if I could catch sight of him, but it was boarded up, sealed tight with a piece of plank and some nails. Margery wasn't kidding when she said John Carder was the meanest person on the planet. *He might be the meanest person in the entire universe, too*, I thought to myself as I followed her into the kitchen.

Before she could ask, I gave her the rundown of what had happened at school. What had turned me from someone who'd wanted to keep her head down and disappear into the crowd into a stark raving lunatic.

"Well, I'm not going to lecture you." Margery rested her hands on the back of a chair. "I'm sure the principal did that already, and it's all stuff you already know. Besides, I have to get back to work. But I do want to tell you something." She hadn't taken off her leather jacket or her leather riding gloves, which stopped at the knuckles and were fastened at her wrists with silver buckles.

I sat down across from her, at the other end of the table. "You want me to leave?"

"No."

"You're going to call Carmella?"

"No."

"Then what?"

Margery stared at the wheel under the table for a few moments. The silence made me nervous, like she was trying to muster the energy to start yelling and screaming. But then she looked up at me. And when she did, I could tell she wasn't going to do either one.

"I had a day like yours once," Margery said. "A long time ago. When I was furious at everyone and everything. I went for a walk to try to blow off some steam, and about a mile down the road, I saw this old, rusty wheelbarrow on the front of someone's lawn. There was a big sign on it that said 'Please Take Me,' so I took it. I didn't know why I took it or what I was going to do with it, but I rolled that darn thing all the way home." She grimaced. "It was heavy, too. And the wheel was broken. Took me over a half hour to get back."

Her face flushed a little as she spoke. She reached up and pulled on one of her earlobes.

"Anyway, I brought it in the house. And I just left it there. I didn't really give it too much thought until a few days later, when, all of a sudden, right out of the blue, it came to me."

"What did?"

"What it wanted to be."

I frowned. She'd had me up to this point. Now I was getting lost. "What do you mean, what it wanted to be? Like it told you?"

"In a way." Margery nodded toward the living room. "Look for yourself. It's sitting right there."

I turned around, scanning the living room. Two blue couches. A green-and-white area rug. Something that looked like a cabinet with two doors filled with small glass panes. A large lamp with a white shade. Next to the lamp . . .

I stood up slowly, examining the strange-looking chair. It had an oddly shaped seat and short, stubby legs. Another set of legs had been drilled into the back to hold it up, but everything else—I could see it now—was the wheelbarrow itself. Margery had even kept the wheel, which stuck out between the front two legs like a little toy. "This is the wheelbarrow?" I looked back at her, wide-eyed.

Margery nodded. "Sit in it," she offered. "It's pretty comfortable."

I settled myself into the bucket seat. She was right. It was wide and spacious, with just enough room on either side for me to cross my arms and legs and sit back a little. "How did you even think of making it into a chair?"

"The first thing I did," Margery said, "was to stop looking at it as a piece of junk. I even stopped looking at it as a wheelbarrow." She shrugged. "The rest just came."

I wasn't sure I understood what she was telling me. But it was pretty cool, whichever way you looked at it.

I ran my hands up and down the metal sides. "How did you get it so smooth? And so red?"

"I had to sand the sides," Margery answered. "I've got a special tool that does that for metal. And then I painted it red."

"It's nice," I said, shaking my head. "It really is."

"I'm glad you like it." Margery took one end of her scarf and tossed it over her shoulder. "Especially since you're going to be sanding and painting a few things of your own for the next two days."

I looked up. "What?"

"You heard me." Margery tucked the ends of her scarf into the front of her leather jacket and zipped it up. "Being suspended from school does not entitle you to a vacation, Fred. You're not going to sit around here twiddling your thumbs for the next forty-eight hours. Come out back with me, and I'll show you what I need you to do."

It almost felt like a trick. Like she'd told me a really crazy story to throw me off-balance so that I'd agree to do whatever she wanted.

Almost.

CHAPTER 10

Margery's metal collection wasn't like anything I'd ever seen before. It was like some kind of crazy playground. There were hubcaps and car doors, something that looked like the back of a refrigerator with thick black coils running up and down the length of it, and an upside-down wok. In the middle of it all, standing watch like an angry giant, was a rusty, rickety structure, complete with wide, slightly concave blades. I couldn't be sure, but it almost looked like the top of a windmill.

"This is all yours?" I asked, sidestepping something that looked like a gigantic wire Slinky.

"Sure is." Margery held open the door to the workshop. "There used to be more but I had to get rid of a lot. It was taking up too much room."

Inside, the workshop was about the size of Margery's kitchen, with a single window on one end and a wide, steeply pitched roof. A table, cluttered with mechanical parts, took up most of the space, and the floor was a carpet of sawdust and metal shavings. It smelled damp, like wet wood, and the air was freezing.

Margery strode over to the table and plucked three items from the mess. Two of them looked like miniature wheels, minus the spokes. The third object was unmistakably a candlestick, except that it was short and chubby. Margery set each item down in front of me and unhooked a long, narrow tool hanging on the wall. "This is a metal sanding bar," she explained. "Watch me first."

I stood close to her as she moved the bar across the outside of the candlestick. Up, down, across. Up, down, across. Dull, flaky chips fluttered to the ground, and Margery's hands disappeared under a pale gray film.

Great, I thought to myself. *This is exactly what I want to be doing over the next two days. Maybe I'll learn how to fall asleep standing up, too.*

But my annoyance vanished as Margery stopped sanding and pointed to the cleanly rubbed section. Gone was the thick, dull veneer. In its place was a smooth portion of something so clean and shiny that it seemed to glow a silvery-rose color.

"What is that underneath?" I asked.

"Looks like nickel." Margery picked it up and examined it more closely. "Maybe lead. Or a titanium metal. Hard to know until it's all done." She handed me the tool. "If you do it right, it will take you the rest of the day to finish this piece. The wheels won't take you nearly as long. You should be able to do both of them tomorrow."

I could feel my heart sinking again. "You seriously want me to stay out here for the rest of the afternoon?"

"I do." Margery looked at me steadily.

"It's freezing."

She walked toward the back of the room and picked up a bulky space heater. "I don't usually bring this out until November, but I guess special circumstances call for special actions." She placed it near the table and plugged the cord into the wall. "It'll take ten minutes or so to really kick in, but just leave it on medium." She pressed the second of three red buttons on top. "Low doesn't do anything, but high gets too hot for such a small area."

"Got it."

"All right, then." She refastened her riding gloves around her wrists. "You're all set."

I got this weird feeling then, and it didn't have anything to do with the fact that I'd gotten in trouble and was being put to work. I sort of didn't want her to leave. Or maybe it was just that I didn't want to be alone. "Are you going to be gone the rest of the day?"

"Yep." Margery looked at her watch. "And I've got to hightail it out of here now, or I'm going to have to stay even later. Factory regulations."

"What time will you be back?"

"Six." She winked at me. "Six ten, if there's any traffic." She reached for a small, portable radio on a shelf above me and fiddled with the knobs. "The time'll fly if you're doing this right, but I like to listen to music while

I'm working." We both listened as the static moved to a man's voice and then to the sudden, happy explosion of music. Beyoncé. I lifted my eyebrows, careful not to show my enthusiasm.

"Yeah?" Margery nodded as I shrugged. "Okay, then." She put the radio back on the shelf. "I'll see you for dinner."

And just like that, she was gone.

It was still too cold to work. I decided to look around until the space heater warmed the place up. The table was a mass of screws and nuts and bolts and car hubcaps and wrenches and silverware, even a rusty bicycle bell. The wall was littered with hooks, each one holding a hammer or a drill or some other kind of tool. There was an entire row of antique skeleton keys, each one hanging by a thin leather cord. I ran my fingers over them and stood there for a moment, watching them sway back and forth in the light. And then in the corner of the workshop, I spotted a green tarp with something blue and purple and a little bit glittery sticking out of one side.

Underneath was the strangest thing I'd ever seen. I guess it was a sculpture of some kind, although honestly it just looked like a bunch of weird items all stuck together. I could make out a rusty kitchen spatula on one side, and an old soup ladle on the other. Something that looked like a clock had been crammed right in the middle.

Nothing about it gave any indication as to what it was. Or what it might become. But apparently, Margery cared enough about whatever it was to protect it.

I arranged the tarp on her project as best I could, straightening the sides and smoothing the edges. Then I walked back over to the worktable in the middle of the room. The small wheels and the candlestick were still there, lined up in a neat little row, waiting for me. It was warm inside now, almost toasty. I took off my jacket and hung it on one of the hooks. Then I sat down on a stool and picked up the sanding bar and went to work.

CHAPTER 11

I'd only been working for an hour or so when Toby started to bark again. My heart sank. He was like an alarm you couldn't turn off. I couldn't hear the music on the radio anymore, and it was getting hard to concentrate. My hands slipped as I moved the sanding bar over the candlestick. It spun out of my hands and fell to the floor.

Woof! Woof! Woof! Woof! Woof! Woof! Woof! Woof!

I'd promised Margery I wouldn't go anywhere near Toby. And I wouldn't. I'd just say something. Loudly, so he could hear me. So that he knew I could hear him.

I grabbed my coat. Outside, the barking was piercing, a steady, repetitive complaint of distress. What was he trying to say? He was probably cold. Maybe even freezing. I wondered if he was hungry, too. Had Mr. Carder bothered to feed him today? Had he even bothered to look at him?

Then, out of the corner of my eye, I saw someone on Margery's porch. I ducked behind a big maple tree and peered around the trunk. A girl who looked very much like Lardvark was standing there, ringing the doorbell. She had on a big army-green coat with fur trim down the front and a white knit hat on her head. Her blond bangs stuck out from the hat like a little shelf. She pushed the doorbell a few more times and looked around. Toby kept barking. Lardvark bit her lip and sighed. She reached out and rang the doorbell a third time.

"Hey!" I stepped out from behind the tree. "You need something?"

She looked so startled—and so overjoyed—to see me that I thought maybe she'd been thinking of someone else. "Oh!" She brought her hands to her cheeks. "You *are* here! I was just about to give up! I thought maybe I got the wrong house, or you'd gone out to do something. Like, in town."

I took a step back as she lumbered down the porch steps and raced up to me. Man, she was eager. A little too eager for my taste. Her cheeks and the tip of her nose were pink from the cold, and she had the most beautiful skin I'd ever seen. It was like marble, with a faint glow about it, like a cloud lit by the sun.

"How are you?" she asked happily.

I frowned. "How'd you know where to find me?"

Her smile faded. "I knew you'd ask me that."

"And?"

"I asked the secretary at school. You know, in the front office. She gave me your address." She winced. "You're not mad, are you? I didn't mean to be nosy or like a stalker or anything. I just . . ." She paused, shaking her head. "We heard that you got a two-day suspension, and I . . . I just couldn't wait."

"Couldn't wait for what?"

"To thank you." Lardvark's eyes were so full of gratitude that for a moment I thought of Toby and the way he'd looked the other night when he was licking my hand.

"What are you talking about? I didn't do anything."

"What're you, nuts?" Lardvark's eyes went wide. "You went flying across that table and beat up Michelle Palmer! All because of me!"

"Okay, first of all, I didn't *beat* anyone up." I shoved my hands inside my pockets. "I got mad at the way that girl pushed you and then the way she talked to me and I pushed her and maybe tried to sit on top of her a little bit, but you know what? I shouldn't have." I shook my head. "I totally should not have done that. It just made everything worse."

Lardvark stood there, staring at me. "But you're wrong," she whispered. "It made everything better."

"I got suspended from school for the rest of the week! How is that better?"

Behind me, Toby started to bark again.

Lardvark pulled on her bottom lip. Her eyes were moist around the edges, and I thought she might cry. "I'm sorry," she said finally. "I meant it made everything better for me."

"For you? How?"

She let go of her lip. "Because . . . well . . . Michelle didn't tap me on the shoulder during science class today."

"What?"

"Michelle didn't—"

"I got that part," I said. "But what does that even mean?"

Toby gave two more barks and then whined. I could hear the chain clinking behind us as he paced back and forth. He was probably dying to know what was going on. Desperate to join us.

Lardvark took a deep breath. "Ever since last year, Michelle has come up behind me in whatever class we have together and tapped me on the shoulder."

"To say hi?" I was thoroughly confused.

"No." Lardvark twisted her fingers. "To let me know, I guess, that she's there. That she's watching me."

"Watching you how?"

Lardvark dragged the toe of her boot through the leaves. "I don't know how to explain it, really. It's just a thing she does. We've never talked about it. But she knows what she's doing. And I know, too. Every day, I sit at my desk in science class and I close my eyes and wait for that little tap. And then it comes, and for a little while, you know, it's kind of over." She shrugged again. "At least for science class."

"*What's* over?"

"Her . . ." She blushed furiously, searching for the words. "I don't know. Her thing over me. You know, like her . . . her . . ."

"Power?" I offered.

"Yeah." Lardvark shrugged, defeated. "Yeah. I guess that's kind of it."

I felt disgusted. For Michelle to do something like that, day after day, week after week, month after month, just because she could was revolting. Absolutely and entirely sickening. But I felt even more disgusted with Lardvark, who allowed it, who sat there every day, quaking in her chair, waiting for that stupid shoulder tap. Why didn't she stand up for herself? She was at least three times bigger than that girl, for crying out loud! She could probably lift Michelle over her head and toss her across the gymnasium if she wanted to.

"Today was the first day she didn't tap me." Lardvark's voice quivered. "Since the beginning of sixth grade. And I know it was because of you. Because you stood up for me in art class. Maybe she knows I have someone now who won't let her get away with it. And I just wanted to find you and come here and tell you that. Because even though you probably think I'm kind of pathetic and everything, I just . . ." She paused, glancing down at the leaves. "I don't know. I guess that's really all I wanted to say."

Toby started barking again as Lardvark turned and walked back down the driveway, her head ducked low, her long arms dipped inside her pockets, and I'm not sure what it was, but something came over me then.

"Wait!" I yelled as she moved farther away. "Hold on a second!"

CHAPTER 12

Lardvark whipped around. Her eyes were wide and round, and inside her pale face, they looked like blue marbles pressed into a mound of soft dough. She stood still as I ran up to her, and for a split second, I saw something like fear flit across her face. "What?" she asked. "I didn't mean—"

"No, no. I just . . ." I shook my head, trying to catch my breath. "I was just wondering if maybe you could do something. You know, for me."

Lardvark's eyes hardened a little and she raised her chin the slightest bit, and it occurred to me that she'd probably been shoved around for a long time. Maybe even longer than Michelle had been in the picture. "Sure," she said casually. "What?"

I pointed back to the fence. "You hear that dog barking?"

Lardvark raised one of her eyebrows. "No, I'm deaf." I grinned a little when she said that, and she did, too.

"Of course I can hear it," she said. "It hasn't stopped barking since I got here. What's wrong with it?"

"He's not being taken care of. He lives with some old guy over there who keeps him chained to a pole and never lets him inside."

"Chained to a pole?" Lardvark's eyes got moist around the corners again. "That's terrible. Why would anyone do that?"

"Because the guy's an awful person." I shrugged. "Because he doesn't care."

"Then why does he keep him?"

"Who knows? The point is, I'm not allowed to go anywhere near Toby. I got in trouble for feeding him the other night, and if I do it again, Margery's going to—" I stopped, catching myself before I said any more.

"Who's Margery?" Lardvark asked.

"A friend of my family's," I said hurriedly. "This is her house. I'm just staying with her for a while." I held my breath, waiting for Lardvark to press me further, but she only said, "So why would she be mad at you for feeding it?"

"*She* doesn't care if I feed him. The guy who owns the dog does. He made a whole stink about it this morning. Said Toby was his property, and I wasn't allowed anywhere near him. He even threatened me."

"Threatened you?" Lardvark looked alarmed. "How?"

"Oh, nothing really. He just said there'd be problems or something like that if I did. You know. But Margery was upset with me. She made me promise I wouldn't go anywhere near him again."

Lardvark raised her right eyebrow again. "So let me guess. You want *me* to feed him?" She was good at moving that one eyebrow. She could arch it up really high without moving the other one. I was impressed.

"Would you?" I dug a fingernail into my palm. "I just can't stand listening to him bark all day long. I know he's hungry."

"I don't know." Lardvark looked down at the ground. "I'm really not a dog person."

"You don't really have to be a dog person to feed one."

"I know. But I really . . . I just don't like to go anywhere near dogs."

"You won't have to go anywhere near him. All you have to do is throw some meat over the fence. You won't have contact with him at all."

Lardvark puffed her cheeks full of air and then blew it out. "What if the owner threatens *me*? I've got enough problems. I don't want to get on some nut's bad side."

"He won't see you. No one will." I stared at her hopefully. "It'll take, like, ten seconds."

Lardvark's eyes swept over my face for a moment, as if considering all the options. She looked pained, as though her stomach hurt. Behind us, Toby barked and barked and barked.

"Okay," she said finally. "I'll do it."

It wasn't hard to find something for Toby to eat. Margery's refrigerator was stocked. There were stacks of thinly sliced turkey and bologna wrapped in white butcher paper, a long stick of hard salami encased in yellow netting, and even a whole baked chicken inside a foil pan, the skin as wrinkled and shriveled as a raisin.

"Holy ravioli!" Lardvark said, peering over my shoulder. "Is Margery some kind of caveman?"

"I don't know what she is." I grabbed the stick of salami and a package of bologna. "She likes to eat, though, that's for sure."

"She likes to eat *meat*," Lardvark observed, following me outside. "It's like a delicatessen in there."

"Okay, now." I pointed to the section of the fence that was nailed over. "Toby can reach to just about there on his chain. So if you throw the meat over there, he'll be able to get it."

"I don't know what kind of aim I have." Lardvark looked nervous all of a sudden as I unwrapped the stack of bologna slices and pushed it into her hand. "I'm not really an athlete."

"You don't have to be." I peeled the netting off the salami stick and shoved it in her other hand. "Just go over there and toss this stuff over. There's no way you can mess it up."

But I was wrong.

Boy, was I wrong.

Lardvark lobbed that meat so far over the fence that even if Toby weren't chained to a pole, he wouldn't have been able to find it. I watched with disbelief as it went sailing far beyond the tree with the yellow leaves and disappeared from sight. I couldn't see Toby, but I could hear the yank and stop of the chain as he started lunging. The sound, combined with the barking, which had reached a new level of desperation, was almost unbearable.

"Ugh!" I kicked the edge of the porch. "Are you kidding me?"

"I *told* you!" Lardvark reached up and yanked the edges of her white hat down around her ears. "I don't have any aim at—" She gasped suddenly and ducked low, covering her head with both hands.

"Now what's wrong?"

"I don't know." Her voice was a whisper. "I thought I heard something break. It sounded like glass."

I thought of the first time I'd seen Toby, how Mr. Carder had been upstairs in the second-floor window, glaring down at me with that shotgun in his arms. There was no way we could risk some other confrontation. "Just come back, then. Come on, forget it. We can—"

"Shhhh!" Lardvark was still crouched down low, but she'd turned her head toward the fence. "Stop talking!"

I watched as she moved closer to the fence and then pressed an ear against one of the slats. What in the world was she doing? Toby's barking had turned into a whine, a high-pitched, pitiful sound that droned on and on. "Oh!" Lardvark hissed. "There it is again!"

"There what is again?" I called from the porch. "More glass?"

"No!" Lardvark looked over at me, her face a map of terror. "It's someone's voice! Inside the house! And it's saying, 'Help me!'"

CHAPTER 13

I thought she was fooling around. Or maybe trying to distract me from the fact that she'd just wasted an entire half pound of German bologna by making up some crazy story.

Then I heard it.

It was hoarse and gravelly and so faint that at first, I thought I was imagining things. But then it came again.

"Help!"

I raced across the lawn, straight toward Lardvark's big eyes and white hat. "Did you hear it?" She clutched at my sleeve. "Did you hear it that time?"

I nodded, rolling up on my tiptoes in an attempt to see over the fence. But it was too high. I took a step back and cupped my hands around my mouth. "Mr. Carder?"

There was no answer.

Lardvark looked up at me in the stillness that followed and then yanked on the leg of my pants. "Why don't we go in and call Margery?" she whispered.

"No way." I shook my leg until she let go. "She already had to leave work early once today because of me. She'll freak out if she has to leave again." I cupped my hands around my mouth a second time. "Hey, Mr. Carder, are you in there?" Still no answer. Even Toby had gotten quiet.

And then, almost as if he was calling from the end of a very long road, we heard Mr. Carder's voice. "Yes! In here! Please help!" It was even fainter than the first time and so weak that I wondered if he had used his last breath to push it out of him.

"We've got to get in there," I said, racing toward the end of Margery's driveway. "Something's happened. He's hurt."

"Well, then, let's call 911!" Lardvark tried to keep up with me, but it was hard for her to run. She sort of loped along for a few seconds and then fell back, waving one arm. "We shouldn't just run into some strange guy's house! Especially someone who's already threatened one of us. What if it's a trap? What if he's just trying to lure you in there?"

I slowed when she said that. My gut told me she was wrong, that even someone like Mr. Carder couldn't make his voice that weak and pathetic-sounding. And how about the fact that his truck was still parked in the driveway? Even Margery had pointed out how strange that was. But now that I thought it all the way through, it made perfect sense. His truck was there because he was still inside.

He'd gotten hurt somehow and hadn't been able to go to work this morning. And no one, except Lardvark and me, knew it.

Still, it was hard to ignore Lardvark's warning, which, combined with Margery's repeated and insistent demands about staying away from Mr. Carder, eventually made me stop walking altogether. Lardvark was right. It would be foolish to go racing inside a strange man's house. There was no telling what we'd find once we got inside— or what we wouldn't.

"How about we just check around outside the house?" Even gasping for breath, Lardvark still managed to look concerned. "For the broken glass."

"What'll that do?"

"Maybe he threw something." I followed Lardvark as she strode past me into Mr. Carder's yard. "Like through a window. You know, to get our attention. And maybe that's where he'll be."

It was a good idea. Actually, it was a great idea. I was a little annoyed that I hadn't thought of it myself. We rounded the corner into Mr. Carder's yard, pushing back dead branches and vines that had collected on one side of the fence. Toby went berserk as we came into view, leaping and pulling so hard on his chain that I thought the pole behind him might come out of the ground. "Shhhh!" I nodded in his direction. "Just hold on a second, buddy. Hold on."

Lardvark grabbed on to me again as we crept around the side of the house. "Are you sure that dog can't get off his chain?"

"Would you stop?" I said, pushing her hand away. "And it's a metal chain. There's no way he can get loose."

A little whimper escaped her mouth, and I felt a pang of guilt. But even without touching me, she was still so close that I could hear her breathing against my neck. "This place is creepy," she whispered.

I couldn't disagree. Mr. Carder's house was an ugly, ramshackle building with a rotting front porch and peeling blue paint. Dead bushes and plants cluttered the edges, and the windows were so dirty they looked almost opaque. But there on the left-hand side, just below a tattered shade . . .

"Look!" I pointed to a jagged hole in the bottom of the first-floor window.

"That must've been the glass I heard breaking," Lardvark said.

I scanned the lawn until I spotted the dark blue coffee mug. It was chipped on the rim, and the handle had broken off, but it was about the same size as the hole in the window. I ran over and picked it up. "What do you think?"

Lardvark inspected the mug, turning it over in her hands. "It must be what he threw." She looked up at me. "Maybe he fell or something. And he's really hurt."

I crept over to the hole in the window and peered inside. It was impossible to see anything beyond it, but an odd smell drifted from the interior. "Mr. Carder?"

Behind us, Toby barked over and over.

"Careful," Lardvark whispered. "Don't get too close yet."

I started to pull back but stopped as a grunting sounded through the hole. I leaned forward again. "Mr. Carder! Are you in there? Are you okay?"

It was impossible to hear his response over the barking. I turned around and looked up at Lardvark. "Will you go see if you can find that bologna you threw? It's the only thing that'll make him be quiet."

Her face blanched.

"You don't have to go anywhere near him," I encouraged her. "Just find the meat and toss it over. You know. Toward him this time."

"Okay." She hurried off, keeping a wide distance between herself and Toby.

I turned back to the window. "Say it again, Mr. Carder! Tell me what's wrong!"

"Hurt!" His voice hovered somewhere between a moan and a gasp. "My neck!"

"The salami!" Lardvark crowed across the yard. She held the stick of meat aloft, like a trophy. "I found it!"

"Well, give it to Toby!"

Lardvark winced. "I don't want to get too close."

I forced myself not to roll my eyes. Man, she was a wimp. An honest-to-goodness cream puff. No wonder she got picked on. She was every bully's dream. "Just roll it toward him," I said. "You know, near enough so he can reach it."

She tipped the salami cautiously in Toby's direction. I held my breath, and the meat stopped just close enough so that Toby could take it in his mouth. He attacked it, biting and snapping and tearing at it.

I turned back to the window. "We're going to get help, Mr. Carder! Don't worry, all right? We're going to call for help and someone will come right away."

"I'm dialing now." Lardvark pulled out a silver iPhone from the pocket of her army-green coat and punched in the number. "Hello, yes? Um . . . our neighbor is hurt." She looked at me and shrugged, but I nodded. "We're not really sure. We haven't been inside the house. But we can hear him through the window. And we're pretty sure he can't get up."

I leaned closer to the window, but it was too dark to see anything. I could hear Mr. Carder's breathing, though, which had shifted into a hoarse, gasping sound. "Tell them to hurry!" I told Lardvark.

There was no way of knowing just how badly Mr. Carder was hurt, but things didn't look good. And I was pretty sure if someone didn't get here fast, it was going to get much, much worse.

CHAPTER 14

It was almost dark by the time the two medics wheeled Mr. Carder out of the house. He lay on a stretcher, wrapped tightly in white blankets, with both arms resting on top. There was a white plastic collar around his neck and a nasty gash on his forehead. Dark blood trickled down one side of his face, and his eyes were closed.

"Oh!" Lardvark gasped when she saw him. "He's not dead, is he?"

"No." The medic at the front of the stretcher shook his head. "But he passed out just a few minutes ago. He got knocked up pretty good in there."

"What's that thing around his neck?" I trotted to keep up with him.

"It's a brace. To keep his neck still. We're not sure yet, but it looks like he might've broken it."

Lardvark gasped a second time. "Do you know what happened?"

"No." The medic nodded to the other one. "One, two, three." Together, the men lifted the stretcher and slid it inside the ambulance. "He was having trouble talking when we found him. And then he fainted. If I had to guess, though, he fell down a flight of stairs. He wasn't too far away from them." He shut the ambulance door. "From the looks of it, he was there for a while, too. At least eight hours."

"Oh!" Lardvark covered her mouth. "That's terrible!"

I shuddered a little thinking of it. If the medic was right, that would mean that Mr. Carder had fallen early this morning, maybe just after I'd gotten picked up by the bus, and then lain there all day. No one deserved that. No matter how mean they were.

"*Fred?*" Margery's voice cut through the darkness as she roared up on her motorcycle. She steered the bike directly across the driveway into Mr. Carder's yard and yanked off her helmet. Her eyes were wide as she strode toward us. "What's going on here? What happened?"

"It's Mr. Carder," I told her quickly. "He fell and broke his neck. At least that's what they think happened. They're taking him to the hospital."

I could see some of the fear drain out of Margery's face as she absorbed my explanation. "Will he be all right?" she asked the medic.

He tapped twice on the closed ambulance door. "We'll

get him there as fast as possible and make sure he gets taken care of. You're not his daughter, are you?"

"No, just a neighbor." Margery sighed heavily. "For the last twenty-seven years."

"Okay." The medic gave us a wave. "We'll try to track down a relative and let them know what's going on." He glanced at Lardvark and me. "You girls did a good job, calling us when you did. Another few hours, and I'm not sure he would have made it."

The three of us watched as the ambulance rolled down Mr. Carder's driveway. The red and blue lights cut large neon swaths through the darkness, and the siren began to wail as it turned onto the main road. Just as the last strains of it faded in the distance, Toby began to howl—long, sad, circular noises that, if I didn't know any better, sounded like crying.

Margery let her head fall back between her shoulders. "Oh Lordy, the dog."

"Can we bring him over here?" The question was out of my mouth before I realized I'd asked it, and Margery looked at me so sharply that I wondered if she'd known I would. "Please? Just for tonight? So he's not all alone?"

"Fred." Margery eyed me steadily. "That dog is probably the closest thing to a wild animal you'll ever see. I can't have him in my house. I just can't. He'll rip everything to shreds."

Toby howled again, and I could tell by the way Margery

clenched her mouth that it was tearing her up inside, too. Just maybe not as much as me.

"So we're going to ignore him?" I glared at her. "Listen to him howl all night?"

"I don't have a choice. I'm sorry."

"What about the shop?" I tried. "Can he stay in the shop, at least?"

"My workshop?"

I nodded. "We can keep a leash on him so he doesn't run around or anything. Maybe put some blankets in there and give him some food, and just . . ." I shrugged. "Just, you know, stay with him for a little bit."

Margery inhaled deeply. Her eyes looked doubtful, and I was sure she was going to find some other reason to say no. But she didn't. "All right. But just for tonight, Fred. I mean it. I don't have the time, space, or energy to care long-term for a dog. Especially this one. Is that clear?"

"Yes!" I was already running toward the fence.

"Hold on a minute!"

I stopped. "What?"

"Don't you have an introduction to make?" Margery tilted her head toward Lardvark, who was just standing there, looking at the ground.

"Oh. Sorry." I walked back over. "This is . . ." But I couldn't remember her real name. I was pretty sure I'd heard the art teacher say it when she'd been taking roll, but now it escaped me. And there was no way I was going to call her Lardvark, which, as far as I was concerned, was one of the meanest, ugliest names I'd ever heard in my life. "Um . . . a girl I met. From school."

"What's your name?" Margery asked.

Lardvark lifted her head the slightest bit and peeked out from beneath her blond bang shelf. "Lardvark," she whispered.

"Pardon?" Margery cocked her head.

I just stared at her.

"Ardelia," Lardvark said, flustered. "My name's Ardelia Lark. But everyone's called me Lardvark since fifth grade."

Margery looked over at me, and I saw something flit across her face. Confusion, maybe? Or was it understanding? "It's nice to meet you, Ardelia." She extended one hand. "You don't have any relation to the Lark and Grove Steel Company in town, do you?"

Lardvark nodded. "It's my dad's."

Margery nodded. "The welding factory I work for gets most of their materials from there."

"That's nice." Lardvark looked over at me.

"Would you like to stay for dinner?" Margery asked.

Lardvark's eyes widened a bit at the invitation. "Really?"

"Sure." Margery shrugged. "I have a great salami in the fridge that I've been waiting to put together with a little pasta and Parmesan cheese. That appeal to you at all?"

Lardvark and I exchanged a quick glance. "Sure." I could hear her suppressing a giggle. "That sounds great."

CHAPTER 15

"You know what's funny?" Lardvark stood a good bit behind me as I made my way over to Toby in Mr. Carder's yard. "I wasn't really sure of your name, either, until Margery said it just now."

I nodded but kept my gaze focused on Toby, who was leaping and jumping all over the place. The closer I got to him, the higher he jumped. His droopy ears rose and fell, slapping the sides of his head, and the chain pulled so tightly against his neck that I could see the pink-and-red sores beneath it. "Okay, buddy," I said softly. "Okay, now. You're going to come with me, but you have to chill out, all right?"

"Is it really Fred?" Lardvark asked. "Your name, I mean?"

"Winifred." I tried to make eye contact with Toby, hoping it might calm him down, but he just bounced around like a crazed Easter bunny. There was no way, once I got the chain off him, that he was going to follow me into Margery's shop. He was too excited. Too wound up. I turned around and looked at Lardvark. "Would you go inside and ask Margery for a leash? I've got to put something around his neck after I take the chain off so that he'll come with me."

"Sure." She turned and vanished into the darkness.

I moved closer to Toby, who was still straining against his chain. "Please, buddy." I held out my hand. "Come on. You've gotta settle down. You just have to. Margery's already nervous about having you over. If you keep acting all crazy like this, she's going to throw you out. She's nice enough, but she has her limits."

I had to hopscotch my way toward him, since most of the ground was littered with poop. There were small indentations, too, where he had dug holes, and I wondered if that was how he amused himself, if maybe that was how he kept from going crazy, tied up to the pole every day like he was. Digging holes in the ground. Maybe looking down into them, waiting for something to look back up.

I got down on my knees and let him jump on me for a minute. But he smelled so terrible that I had to push him away again. His toenails, which were as long as toothpicks, tore at my clothing, and chunks of dried mud fell from his fur in clumps. I stood back up. "I'm sorry, buddy. It's nothing personal. I swear it isn't." I tried to keep petting his head, but he lunged as I got back up, desperate to touch me again. "It's okay, Toby. I'm right here." I could feel my throat tightening. "I'm not leaving."

"Margery had a rope!" Lardvark waved a white coil above her head as she jogged toward me. She stopped about halfway across the yard and threw it in my direction. Toby's big eyes watched as the rope went sailing past him and his shed and landed near the bushes at the back of the yard. He paused for a second and then dashed toward it.

"Oh!" Lardvark covered her mouth with her hands. "Holy guacamole."

"Man, you weren't kidding when you said you had no aim." I rolled my eyes. "You've got to stop throwing things." I started to move toward the back of the yard but stopped as Toby bolted in our direction, the rope dangling from his mouth. I just stood there, staring, as he bounded toward me and dropped it at my feet.

"Is that the rope?" Lardvark called.

"Yes!" I knelt down again and petted Toby's head. Maybe he *was* trained. Or had been, at some point. He certainly wasn't wild, like Margery had said. "Good boy. What a good boy you are, Toby." He licked my hands and arms and the outside of my coat. He didn't stop even when I tried to pull the chain off his neck and it stuck because of the dried blood and hair attached to it.

Maybe I let my guard down a little after that. Or maybe I gave Toby too much credit after seeing him fetch the rope. One thing was for sure: I definitely underestimated how strong he was. And how fast. Because as soon as I got that chain off his neck and slipped on the rope, he bolted. I grunted as the rope cut into my hand, and when Toby yanked on the other end, my shoulder just about dislocated from the socket. It hurt too much not to let go. I ran after him, yelling and screaming, but he was too fast.

And as Lardvark and I watched, Toby raced across Mr. Carder's yard, through Margery's, and disappeared into the woods.

CHAPTER 16

"What do you mean, he's gone?" Margery wiped her hands on a dish towel and stalked out of the kitchen. "Gone where?"

"I don't know!" I fought down a rising panic in my chest. "I barely got the rope around his neck, and he just ran!"

"Well, of course he ran." Margery snatched her leather jacket off a hook on the wall and tossed it over her shoulders. "What would you do if someone let you off a chain you'd been tied to for the last ten years?"

Lardvark and I followed her down the front steps, then stopped abruptly as she wheeled back around again. "I can't see a thing out here," she muttered. "Hold on a minute while I get us some flashlights." I winced as she slammed the door behind her, and shoved my hands in my pockets. This was the last thing she needed.

"Do you think Mr. Carder will be upset with us?"

Lardvark was wringing her hands. "I mean, if we can't find him?"

I was glad it was dark, because I could feel my face pale at Lardvark's question. I hadn't even thought of Mr. Carder's reaction to his missing dog. Nor had the possibility of not finding Toby entered my mind. Now, considering both, I felt sick to my stomach. "We'll find him," I said firmly. "He knows his name. We're just going to call and call until he comes back." I shrugged. "How far could he go, really?"

Lardvark looked at me, and I knew she was thinking the same thing. Toby could go as far as he wanted now that he was free. He could probably run all the way to Philadelphia if he tried. And who would blame him? If I were him, I'd run so far away from Mr. Carder that he'd never find me again. If only Toby could've been a little like that bird in our apartment in Philadelphia, weighing what he'd be giving up first before flying away. But maybe he didn't have to. Maybe he already knew.

I closed my eyes and forced myself not to think about it.

"All right." Margery banged the door back open, tossing a flashlight to me and one to Lardvark. "Which direction did he run in, Fred?"

I pointed to the woods on the other side of Margery's yard.

"The woods." Margery's shoulders sagged. "Of course

he did. Well, let's get started. I think it would be smartest if we split up. All three of us looking in the same direction will just be a waste of manpower. Fred, why don't you go left? Ardelia, you go right. And I'll go straight down the middle." She paused, glancing at Lardvark. "Hold on. Did you call your parents to let them know you're staying for dinner?"

Lardvark looked startled for a moment and then nodded. "Yeah," she said. "Yeah, I called them just now."

I looked at her strangely. The only call she'd made was to 911 about Mr. Carder. Why was she lying?

"Okay." Margery squared her shoulders. "As long as they know where you are. A missing animal is one thing. I'm not going to be responsible for a missing kid, too." She looked at her watch. "It's six thirty. We'll look for Toby for a half hour. Yell if you find him. Otherwise, we'll all meet back here at seven. Deal?"

I pushed Lardvark's weird behavior to the back of my mind. Finding Toby was the most important thing right now. "Hold on." I raced over into Mr. Carder's yard, aiming my flashlight toward the bushes where Lardvark had lobbed the meat. It didn't take long for me to make out the packet of bologna, which was shoved deep inside the bush itself. Toby wasn't going to get away from me this time. Not if I had a stack of fresh meat to woo him home with. I grabbed the package quickly and ran back.

"Let me guess," Margery said, turning her flashlight on the white butcher paper package. "That's my good German bologna."

I nodded.

"And I suppose the salami has gone by the wayside, too?" She rubbed her chin as she shifted the flashlight to my face. "Or are you hiding that for another time?"

I dropped my eyes.

"But Fred didn't give it to Toby," Lardvark said hastily. "She told me all about you not wanting her to have contact with the dog and she didn't. Not once."

"Mmmm-hmmm." Margery moved her beam of light off me. "We can talk about this later. Let's get going before it gets any darker. Everybody remember the direction they're moving in?"

Lardvark and I nodded. We followed Margery across the yard, staying a few steps behind her as she plunged through the middle of the woods.

"See you in a bit." I turned left, where Margery had directed me to go. To my relief, I could make out a rough path snaking through the brush. It would be easy to follow. "Just hang on to that rope if you find him. And then scream and holler." I paused for a moment, waiting for Lardvark to answer.

But she didn't.

And she didn't turn right, where Margery had told her to go.

"What's the matter?" I asked.

"I . . . I can't go into those woods by myself." Her voice was soft.

"Sure you can," I told her. "You have a flashlight. And they're not really woods. It's more just—"

"It doesn't matter." She shook her head. "It's still too dark. I can't do it. Not by myself."

I stared at her for a moment as she fingered the edge of her coat. Man, oh *man*. This girl needed to get a backbone. Take some karate lessons or something.

"Please," she said. "Please, can I just come with you?"

"I guess you'll have to." I started walking. "Come on."

CHAPTER 17

We followed the trail back to Margery's house in silence. Thirty long minutes of yelling and searching hadn't brought Toby home. I felt sick to my stomach, thinking about how angry Mr. Carder would be when he heard the news about his dog. And more importantly, poor Toby was all alone out there in the dark. Where would he find shelter? Food? How would he stay warm? It wouldn't be a huge stretch, after being left outside for so long at Mr. Carder's house, but it would still be hard. He wouldn't know anything. Or anyone.

Just before we reached the end of the trail, Lardvark turned and looked at me. "Can I ask you a question?"

I knew what was coming. "I guess."

"Why are you staying with Margery?" she asked. "Did something happen to your parents?"

I shrugged, trying not to show my irritation. "It's complicated," I said. "And it's kind of personal. I don't really want to talk about it."

"I'm sorry," Lardvark said. "I can be nosy at times. I don't mean to be."

I nodded, waving as Margery appeared up ahead. Her face was grim as she flicked off her flashlight. "Okay, girls, we've done what we could do for now. We'll look again tomorrow. Let's go eat."

We went inside. And maybe it was because I was tired. Or cold. Or maybe it was the click of the door behind me, which kind of signaled once and for all that we hadn't found Toby, who was missing now because I hadn't been able to hang on to his stupid rope. Whatever it was, I found myself clenching my teeth. I wanted to hit something. Or someone.

Instead, I turned on Lardvark. "Why'd you lie before about calling your parents?"

Margery stopped taking off her leather jacket, one arm still in the sleeve.

Lardvark's face paled. "I didn't lie."

"Yes, you did." I could feel my anger building, a spark catching. "You told Margery you called them when she was inside. But you didn't call anyone."

Margery walked toward us. "Your parents don't know you're here?"

Lardvark bit her lip. She stared at the floor and shifted on one foot.

"Please answer me." Margery's voice was so stern that even I felt a little nervous.

Behind us, in the kitchen, the phone rang. Margery blinked. "I am going to answer this phone, and when I get back, I would like an answer." She pointed a thick finger at Lardvark. "An honest one this time."

Lardvark raised her head as Margery disappeared from the room. Her eyes were wet. "Why would you do that?"

"Why would you lie?" I shot back. "Especially about something like that? That's just dumb."

"You don't know anything," Lardvark whispered.

"Fred!" Margery's voice drifted out from the kitchen. "It's for you!"

Me? Who would be calling me?

"Fred!"

I walked into the kitchen, leaving Lardvark behind. The weird thing was, ratting her out hadn't made me feel better. In fact, I just felt angrier. And what did "you don't know anything" mean?

Margery held out the receiver.

"Who is it?" I asked.

"Your mother," she said. "And she says she only has five minutes. Come on, take it."

CHAPTER 18

"Mom?"

"Sweetie! Hi! How are you?"

As Margery left the kitchen to give me some privacy, I sat down so that my legs wouldn't give out beneath me. "I'm okay. How are you?"

"I'm all right. Tired, mostly. It's hard to sleep in here. It gets pretty noisy at night."

I lowered my voice. "So you're still in . . ." But I couldn't bring myself to say it out loud. I just couldn't do it.

"Yeah, I'm still here. I couldn't post bail. You know what bail is, right?"

"The money you have to pay to get out of there?"

"Right. I don't have it, so I have to wait in here until my hearing." She sighed. "It's okay, though. I'm trying to make the most of it. You know, just like I've always told you. Make the most of things, or things will make—"

"The most of you," I finished.

She laughed softly. "Exactly."

"Mom, what happened? Why did they arrest you?"

"Oh, they thought I stole some pills." She sighed again. "To be fair, it kind of looked like I did. I was helping out the pharmacist—you know how I sometimes do? And she asked me to go put the pill bottles into the baskets lined up in the back. There were a few, though, that needed to go in the front, so I put them in my pocket so I wouldn't forget them and . . . Oh, honey, it was so stupid. I just wasn't thinking."

I *knew* it.

They'd gotten it all wrong. Mom would never have stolen pills. It had all been a huge mistake. But there was still something I didn't understand. "If it was just an accident, then why'd they put you in jail?"

"Because they don't believe it was an accident yet. But I'll get to tell them everything at my hearing. It won't be long." She took a breath. "How about you? They told me you're staying with a really nice woman named Margery?"

"Yeah." I studied the metal chair across the table from me. Counted the petals along one of the flowers etched into the back of it. One. Two. Three. Four. Five. "She lives in Lancaster."

"Oh, honey," Mom said. "That's over an hour away! Why so far?"

"I don't know. That's just how it turned out, I guess."

"Well, how is it? She's being nice to you, right?"

"Yeah." I paused. "She rides a motorcycle. That's what we rode on back to her house."

"You had a helmet on, I hope."

"Yeah. A big, heavy one. It was kind of exciting, actually."

"I bet it was. What else is she like?"

"Well, she's pretty tall." I paused. "And she works at a welding factory in town, I think. She's a good cook, too."

Mom sighed. "I'm sorry that didn't run in the family. I do wish I knew how to cook better."

I felt a rush of emotion then, and I bit my lip to hold it back. "I miss you, Mom."

"I miss you, too, angel. More than you know. But don't worry. We'll be together soon." Her voice quavered a little. "Which reminds me. I need to ask you something."

The way her voice rose made my Mom radar flick on. "Okay," I said carefully.

Mom took a deep breath. "I'm not sure if you know this yet, but after my hearing about the pills is over, there'll be another one, about you and me."

My heart sped up. "Why?"

"Some judge will have to determine whether or not you can come back and live with me."

"Wait, why wouldn't I?"

"Oh, you will. It'll be fine." Mom paused. "But he's probably going to ask you some things."

"What kind of things?"

"Well, about me. You know. At home."

I could feel my armpits start to sweat. My stomach flipped over and then back again, and I wondered if I would throw up right there on Margery's kitchen floor. "What do they need to know?" I managed to say.

Mom took another deep breath. "They'll want information about me that only you can give." She paused again, and in that moment, I knew what she was going to ask me.

"Like what?" I asked anyway.

"Like if you've ever seen anything other than the pills I get from the doctor. You know, at the apartment."

I closed my eyes tight. And then tighter still until the little plastic bottle I'd once found inside the pocket of Mom's jean jacket disappeared.

"Fred? If you just wouldn't mention anything about that part . . ."

"I'd never tell them that."

"No?" Mom's voice wobbled.

"No." I stood up. "That's no one's business."

"Okay." She sniffed, and I could tell she was fighting back tears. "Because it'll change everything if you do, sweetie. Everything. I promise you that I will do better. I'll go to meetings and do whatever I need to get well. For you. For us. I just . . ." I could hear her choke down a sob. "I just can't do it without you. You're my whole life. My home. My heart." She blew her nose, and when she was finished, her voice sounded different. Steadier. "Listen, how about once this is all over, we move out of Philadelphia and go somewhere fresh and start over? Just the two of us. It'll be a whole new chapter. A whole new life. Somewhere far away, in a brand-new place."

I stared at the petals on the flower again while she talked. One. Two. Three. Four—

"Fred?"

"Yeah." I nodded, thinking of our new life together up ahead. A whole new city. New neighbors and a new school and a new job for Mom, who would be healthy and happy again. It would be great. It would. "Yeah, it sounds awesome, Mom."

"Oh, honey." She gave another quavering sigh. "Oh, you don't know what this means to me. Thank you so much. I don't know what I'd do without you." I could hear a man's voice yelling behind her. "Oh, sweetie, I have to go, okay? My time's up. They're going to cut me off. I love you."

"I love you, too, Mom."

"I love you three." She choked back another sob.

"I love you four."

"I love you more."

And just like that, the phone went dead.

CHAPTER 19

It was hard to know if Margery had been eavesdropping, or if she just picked the right time to come back in the kitchen. Either way, two seconds after I hung up the phone, she appeared, smoothing down the hair on top of her head with her palms. Her cheeks were pink, and her lips looked dry and chapped.

"Everything go okay?" she asked.

"Yeah." My brain felt fuzzy, like it was underwater. Had Mom said when the second hearing would be? A week? Two weeks? What if the judge didn't believe what I told him? I wasn't very good at lying. My voice shook. I had trouble keeping eye contact. Maybe I'd practice. Look in the mirror in my room and say what I needed to say out loud a few times. *My mother only takes the medicine the doctor gives her. No, I've never seen anything else. Not once. Never.*

"I took your friend home," Margery said, yanking the refrigerator door open. "I don't know what her story is, but she cannot come back here again unless I talk to her mother or father myself and hear that they are okay with her being here."

I looked around, as if Margery might be playing a trick on me, but Lardvark was gone. "I didn't hear you leave."

Instead of answering, Margery reached farther into the refrigerator.

"Did you take her home on the bike?"

"Yep." Margery stepped back from the refrigerator. Her arms were filled with little plastic containers covered with blue and green lids. "It took a few minutes to figure out where to put the unicycle, but she—"

"Unicycle?" I interrupted. "What unicycle?"

"Her unicycle." Margery dropped the containers on the table. "You didn't know she had a unicycle? How do you think she got over here?"

I tried to remember the moment Lardvark had first arrived. I hadn't thought to ask how she'd gotten here. It hadn't even occurred to me. But a unicycle? *Really?*

"Anyway," Margery said, "she doesn't live very far. Two, three miles tops. I was there and back in five minutes. You and your mother were just saying your goodbyes when I came back in."

I could feel the heat rise to my cheeks as I thought of her listening to Mom's and my parting ritual. That was private. Something just between us. "I'm going upstairs."

Margery sat down. "Not until you eat something."

"I'm not hungry."

"You're starving," Margery said. "I can see it in your face." She patted the spot at the table where I'd been sitting. "Sit down. Let's go through these leftovers and see what looks appealing."

"I told you—"

"I know what you told me." Margery leveled her eyes at me and held my gaze. "It's the least you can do after giving my good soppressata salami to the dog. That was supposed to be our dinner tonight."

I plopped down. Man, she was good at playing that guilt card. I stared at the table as she started peeling lids off the containers.

"So how'd you and this Ardelia girl meet?" Margery sniffed the contents of one container and then put it back down.

"At school."

"Where? At lunch? Gym?"

"Art class."

Margery nodded, sniffing another container. This time, she made a face. "Phew." She stood up and chucked it into the garbage. "That one has seen better days, I'm afraid." She walked back over and sat down. "How'd she end up here? Did you invite her over?"

"Nope. She just showed up." I paused. "On her unicycle, apparently."

"Why?"

"I have no idea."

"No idea?" Margery nodded as she inspected another container. "Chicken Parmesan. Still good. I can heat this up in two seconds and throw it over a plate of hot pasta."

I didn't answer.

"People don't usually just show up at someone's house for no reason," Margery said. "Why was she here?"

"Because she's weird," I said. "I don't know."

Margery studied me for a minute. I could tell she was doing that thing where she was deciding what to say next. It made me a little nervous again, as if she was trying to figure out parts of me I hadn't told her about yet. "Okay." She got up out of her chair. "You don't want to tell me—that's your right. I won't push." She unhooked a large saucepan from the hanging rack above her and set it on the stove. "How 'bout your mother? How's she?"

"Fine."

"Good. Glad to hear it."

"She wanted to know about you." I sat up, a little startled. I hadn't known I was going to say that.

"I'm sure she did." Margery turned on the flame on the stove and dumped the chicken Parmesan into the saucepan.

"I told her about your motorcycle."

Margery nodded, stirring the sauce with a big wooden spoon. "Was she okay with that?"

"Surprised, mostly. She wanted to know if I wore a helmet."

"That's because she's a good mother."

I glanced over at her sharply, wondering if she was being sincere. "She is a good mother," I said. "She's actually a great mother."

"I'm sure she is." Margery looked over at me and nodded. "And you're a good kid." I looked down at the table, unsure how to respond. "You know, Ardelia told me something just before I dropped her off."

I didn't answer. I didn't want to talk about Ardelia or Lardvark or whatever she wanted to be called.

"Do you want to know what it was?"

"No. But you'll tell me anyway."

Margery smiled faintly. "It was about you."

"Great."

"She said that you are the nicest person she's ever met."

"Awesome."

"That's not all."

I bit the inside of my cheek.

"She said she felt like she met you for a reason. And that something in her life is about to change because of it."

I wanted to cry just then. I really, really did. Mostly because I could hear the hope in Lardvark's words. And because she was wrong. She was completely, 100 percent wrong about me. "I told you she's a weirdo," I heard myself say. "Seriously. She's kind of out there."

"I don't think she's weird at all," Margery said. "I think she's kind of a cool cat, myself. I doubt there's too many twelve-year-olds who know how to ride a unicycle.

And I think she might be right about meeting you for a reason."

I rolled my eyes and rose. "That's because you don't know anything."

"Oh, I know—" Margery's eyes widened as she stopped talking. "Hold on a second. You hear that?"

"Hear what?"

"Listen!"

We stood there, straining our ears in the silence together. And then I heard it, too. The sound was faint at first, like a call in the distance. But it got stronger, until it could've been coming from just outside the door. "Hello!" it barked. "Here I am again!"

Toby.

CHAPTER 20

He was just sitting there in front of the porch steps, looking up at us like a goofy little kid. The rope I'd slipped
around his neck trailed off behind him like an after-
thought. His mouth was open and his tongue hung out as
he panted, and if I didn't know any better, I would have
said he was grinning at us.

"Well, I'll *be*." Margery shook her head as we stood
in the doorway. "He went and found his own way back."

Toby barked once, as if agreeing with her.

I lunged for him, but she pulled me by the arm. "Not
yet. He'll run again if he thinks you're going to grab
him. Where's that bologna you brought with you in the
woods?"

I reached inside the front pocket of my hoodie and
pulled it out. "Right here."

"Good." Margery watched Toby as she spoke. "Put a
little bit here on the porch and let's see what happens."

I peeled off a few slices and rolled them up. "Food, Toby," I said gently, holding them out in his direction. His nose quivered. "Come and get it, boy." I set the bologna down in front of me and patted the porch floor with my hand. "Come on, Toby. I know you're hungry."

He whined, and I could tell he wanted the meat but that he was afraid to come any closer. I knew why, too. He'd just tasted something more delicious than any piece of bologna. Running out there all by himself, he got to feel the cold air ripple through his fur and the crunch of dry leaves under his paws, and he didn't want to lose it again. No matter how hungry he was.

I knelt down, just behind the bologna. "Toby. Come and eat, buddy. It's okay."

He watched me with his big eyes. Some of the gooey stuff around his eyelids was gone, but they were still red-rimmed and swollen. He cocked his head, as if considering my words, and his nostrils flared. I pushed the bologna a little farther out on the porch. His nose quivered again and this time, when he whined, it ended in a single, short bark.

"You can trust me." I nodded. "I promise I won't hurt you."

Toby's hindquarters shuddered as he sat up straight. He reached out a paw and pulled himself onto the bottom step. I pushed the bologna out again. He lifted his other paw and took another step. And then, before I could take a breath, he was all the way up on the porch, hunched over the meat. Behind me, Margery squatted down quickly and took hold of the rope. "Give him some more," she said, nudging me. "Quick, before he realizes I've got the rope."

I shoved more bologna under Toby's nose. As he wolfed down seconds, and then thirds, I had to turn my face to the side again because he smelled so bad, but I kept petting him and telling him what a good boy he was. And I didn't stop, not even after he finished the whole package of meat and realized that Margery was holding the other end of the rope. He tensed once—probably thinking of running—but I looked at him directly and shook my head, and I kept petting that sad little bald spot on top of his head, and suddenly, as if the batteries inside him had stopped working, he gave a long, trembling sigh and lay down next to me.

"We're going to have to give him a bath," Margery said. "The smell on him is revolting."

"It's not his fault." I was still petting Toby's head. I wondered if the bald spot would get any bigger if I petted it enough.

"I didn't say it was." Margery uncoiled the rope from around her hand. "But there's no way in heaven he's going to stink up my shop. I'll never be able to work in there again." She handed me the rope. "You stay here with him, and I'll get what we need to scrub him down. I'll yell for you when I'm ready."

I wrapped the rope around my hand the way Margery had done, but it didn't look as though I was going to have to worry about Toby bolting a second time. His head lay on the floor, arranged neatly between his paws, and his eyelids were heavy, as if he might fall asleep at any minute.

"You tired, buddy?"

He thumped his tail against the porch.

"You should be. You probably just had the run of your life out there, didn't you?" I leaned in a little bit. "Where'd you go? You see anything really cool? Anything you want to tell me about?"

Toby lifted his head when I said that, and when he looked at me, I could've sworn I saw a glint in his eyes that said yes, he had seen something. He'd seen some of the world beyond the horrible little patch of mud and dirt he'd been chained to for the last ten years. And even though it was small, it was clean and pure and green and glorious.

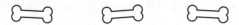

"Don't let him in the tub yet," Margery ordered. "But hold tight to the rope. I've got to hose him down first. Get that first layer of dirt off him." She wrinkled her nose. "And maybe the second or third."

I bent down close to Toby's ear. It was the one that was only half an ear, a sad little flap matted heavily with dirt. I hoped it worked, that he could still hear out of it okay. "All right, buddy," I said softly. "This might be scary at first, but it's just water. Like rain kind of, okay? It's nothing to be afraid of. Try to stay real quiet and still. I'll be right here. And then after she's done, you can jump into that warm, sudsy tub over there and we'll scrub you down." I stroked the top of his head. "Can you do that for me, buddy? Just for a little bit?"

"Okay?" Margery asked as I straightened up again. "He ready?"

I nodded, retightening my grip on the rope. "Go ahead."

Margery didn't turn the water on very hard, but it came out forcefully enough to start dislodging some of the mud chunks embedded in Toby's fur. He gave a startled bark when the water first made contact, and leaped high into the air.

"Hold him tight!" Margery bellowed. "Don't let go!"

"It's okay, Toby!" I called, wrapping the rope around my wrist a third time. I gasped as it cut into the skin, and used my other hand to loosen some of the slack. "Toby, it's all right! Stay still, buddy! It won't take long!"

"I don't know about that." Margery looked grim as she aimed the hose at Toby's belly. "I doubt Carder's ever given this poor animal a washing."

I wasn't sure how much longer my wrist was going to be able to take the tear and pull of the rope. For such a small, underfed dog, Toby was strong. Or at least much stronger than my arm.

But suddenly, without any warning, he stopped jumping. He stood there instead, with his head hanging low and his tail tucked in between his legs, as Margery finished hosing him down.

It was almost as if he'd quit, I thought later. Given up a fight he knew he couldn't win.

Or maybe it was something else. Something I didn't know about yet.

Couldn't know about, until the same thing happened to me.

CHAPTER 21

I hardly recognized Toby after his bath. His black-and-white fur shone under the light of the back porch, and his ears—even the sad little half one—were all soft and floppy. Margery found a wire cutter inside the work shed and clipped his toenails, but only after she'd used a pair of sewing shears to trim the hair around them. She used the shears to trim the straggly hair under his belly and along the backs of his legs, too, and wiped all the goo out of his eyes, and if Toby had started out looking like a sloth that had rolled in the mud, now he looked like a dog. A real, honest-to-goodness dog.

I couldn't stop hugging him, and he seemed happy, too, because he kept pushing his head into me and licking my face. Even Margery seemed pleased. She made a big deal about cleaning up the porch, and she groused about how dirty everything had gotten, but I noticed her watching us out of the corner of her eye a few times.

And I saw her smile.

She stopped smiling, though, when I stood back up and Toby jumped on me. "Don't let him do that anymore," she said. "Jumping on people isn't good dog behavior."

I rubbed Toby behind the ears and down along his neck. "Why not?"

"It teaches him he can do anything." Margery shook her head. "And if a dog thinks he can do anything, he'll do whatever he wants."

"He should be able to do whatever he wants." I leaned down closer to him, nuzzling my nose into his neck. "He hasn't been able to do anything in forever."

"It doesn't work that way." Margery dumped the aluminum tub over. The suds were long gone, and the water that gushed out over the side was a deep brown color. "Dogs need direction. If they don't have it, they don't know how to act. And when you've got a dog on your hands that doesn't know how to act, you're going to find yourself in over your head. Next time he jumps up on you, grab his paws and squeeze them. Not hard, but firmly. Dogs are very protective of their paws. They know if something happens to them, they'll be in trouble. He'll get the message."

I paused for a moment, watching the last of the dirty water drain out of the basin. "Did you ever have a dog?"

"I did." Margery righted the basin and heaved it against one hip. "A long time ago."

"What happened to him?"

"He died." A muscle pulsed in Margery's cheek. "Why don't you bring Toby inside the shop? We'll figure out where he'll be most comfortable and then set up a bed for him."

I wanted to ask her if she'd been the one to train her dog, and if she had, where she'd learned to do such a thing. But it was late. And I could tell by the way she kept putting her hands on her lower back and leaning into them that she was getting tired.

"How about here?" Margery pointed to a cleared-out spot a little ways from the heater. "He'll be warm enough, I think, but not too warm."

"It looks perfect," I said happily. "What do you think, Toby?"

Toby barked. He looked at me and then over at Margery, and I knew that if he could have talked, he would have said something like thank you. Not just for cleaning him up and taking him in, but for seeing him before he'd been clean.

For seeing him and wanting him anyway.

He seemed confused by the pile of blankets we showed him, lifting a paw and touching the edge of one gently, as if it might be hot.

"Go ahead," I encouraged him. "Those are for you. You can lie down on them and go to sleep."

He looked up at me with a perplexed expression and wagged his tail.

"Why don't you show him?" Margery said.

"Me?"

"It's you or nothing. I'm not getting down there. I won't be able to get back up."

Toby watched as I got down on my hands and knees and crawled onto the pile of blankets. "See?" I told him. "Just like this." I curled up on one side and tucked an arm under my head. "This is how I sleep, but you can lay any way you like. Whatever's comfortable." I motioned with my fingers. "Come on over, buddy." I patted the blankets with my hand. "You can lie down right here. There's lots of room."

Toby's eyelids drooped. I bet he knew sleep was just around the corner—if only he would let it come. He put a paw up against the edge of the blankets, and this time, he followed it with the other one, until he was all the way inside the tangle of soft material. He settled himself slowly, lowering his hindquarters and then his front legs, and finally dropping his head. He thumped his tail once, briefly, and gave a long sigh. And then he closed his eyes. In less than a minute, he was snoring.

"He's a good dog," I said, running my hand down his back.

"All dogs are good," Margery said. "Or at least they start out that way. It's people that turn them mean."

I nodded, thinking of Mr. Carder. Had he been

neglectful of Toby on purpose? Or was he just too old to give a dog the time and the attention it deserved?

I hoped it was the second option, but I wasn't too sure.

And maybe, now that Toby was with us, it didn't matter anyway.

CHAPTER 22

"I'm going to swing by the hospital after work and see how Mr. Carder's doing," Margery said the next morning. She'd knocked on the shed door to let me know she was coming in, but Toby and I had been awake for over an hour. I'd stayed with him through the night, worried that he would wake up and be frightened by his new surroundings, but he'd slept all the way through. Since then, however, he hadn't stopped moving, darting this way and that, as far as the rope around his neck would allow, and sniffing every single thing he could find. He'd peed once, too, lifting a hind leg in a corner before I spotted him and realized what he was doing. I'd mopped it up as best I could, but a small dark stain remained. I hoped Margery wouldn't notice.

"What if Mr. Carder asks about Toby?" I took the blue mug Margery held out to me. "What will you tell him?"

"I'll tell him the truth." Margery placed a bowl of raw hamburger meat next to Toby. She petted him gently as he bent over it and wolfed it down. "That Toby's over here with us."

I stirred the contents of my mug. It looked like oatmeal, but there were other things mixed in there, too. Cranberries, maybe. And walnuts. It smelled good. "What if Mr. Carder gets mad?"

"Then he gets mad. I'll deal with it. It's not like he's going to come storming back here anytime soon. My guess is he'll be in the hospital for a while."

"Who's going to take care of him?" I shoved a spoonful of the oatmeal in my mouth. It tasted as good as it smelled. "Mr. Carder, I mean. After he comes back home?"

"Let's not get ahead of ourselves." Margery stood up and buckled one of her riding gloves. "We don't even know how seriously injured he is yet. How's the oatmeal?"

I nodded, and since my mouth was still full, gave her a thumbs-up.

"Good." Margery reached over and straightened my three projects on the worktable. "Since you've got the whole day, I expect all of these to be sanded when I get home. All right?"

I nodded. "Can I take a few breaks, though? Maybe let Toby walk around on the rope and get some fresh air?"

"He's not going to walk anywhere on that rope." Margery knotted her scarf and tucked it inside the front of her jacket. "As soon as his feet hit the ground, he's going to run like he did yesterday. I don't know about you, but I'm not interested in spending another evening poking around in the woods, looking for him. Take him out once or twice so he can relieve himself, but tie him to the stoop there. When he's done, bring him right back in. And remember what I told you about letting him jump up on you." She held up both hands. "Paws."

"Paws." I nodded. "Gentle, but firm."

"Exactly." Margery gave me a short salute. "I've got to go or I'll be late. Have a good one, Fred." She closed the door, only to open it again. "Oh, and I made you a sandwich for lunch. Turkey with cheese. It's on a plate wrapped in Saran wrap on the kitchen table. There's potato chips in the pantry, too, and lemonade in the fridge."

"Thanks." I made a hopeful face.

"No, the dog cannot have any of the turkey." Margery's voice was firm. "Or anything else in the refrigerator."

My face fell.

"I chopped up some more hamburger and put it in a bowl for him." She winked at me. "It's just inside the kitchen door."

I grinned and gave her another thumbs-up. "Thanks."

Toby whined as Margery disappeared, and began straining toward the door. "You just peed," I reminded him. "I'll let you out in a while." He whined again, a small, pitiful sound that broke my heart a little. I knew he wanted to run, especially since he'd gotten a taste of it after so long. But I couldn't risk him bolting again. The fact that he'd found his way back last night was a miracle. But everyone knew that miracles were one in a million.

I sighed as he kept whimpering. Maybe I could meet him halfway. Figure out a compromise that would make both of us happy. I knelt down in front of him and ran my hand over his head. "Will you be a good boy in here if I take the rope off? You can poke around and explore all you want then. You want to do that? Huh?"

Toby sat back on his haunches as I touched him. He stared at me with his brown eyes and barked once. It sounded like a yes to me. "Okay, then." I slipped the rope from around his neck and waited, holding my breath. I expected him to dart off instantly, the way he'd done outside. But he didn't. He stepped into me instead and nuzzled his head against my chest. Then he looked up and licked my cheek. His tongue was warm, and his breath smelled like hamburger, but I didn't pull away. I knew he was thanking me. And that he would try to be good because I had given him this one small thing.

"Oh, Toby." I rubbed my hands up and down his sides. I could feel his ribs under his newly clean fur, and the bones in his hips. "Okay, buddy. It's okay."

I worked for a while after that, sanding the candlestick as Toby nosed around the corners. I let him out once to do his business, but afterward, he kept going to the door and scratching to get out again. "No, Toby," I'd say each time, shaking my head. "Not now." He'd stare at me for a minute, as if deciding whether or not to argue, and then go back to sniffing and nosing and exploring anything within reach.

But even with music playing low in the background, and Toby poking around, it was quiet in there. Too quiet.

It reminded me of our apartment back in Philadelphia, especially on Saturday afternoons, when the sun would slant through the window and Mom would disappear into the bedroom. I could hear all the noises of the city out-side our window—horns blaring and brakes screeching, people yelling, and doors slamming—and yet when that bedroom door closed, it was like all the sound had been sucked out of the room.

So when the quiet in the shop got to that point, and my skin started to prickle, I went over and turned up the radio. Rihanna was singing a song about someone who had hurt her and how even taking a breath was painful. I cranked up the volume to five, then eight, and then twelve, which was the loudest it would go. Toby lifted his nose out of a corner he'd been sniffing and turned his head. I could see his ears twitch a little as the music got louder, and then he went perfectly still as it got even louder than that. His tail stopped moving, and he watched me care-fully. It was like he was waiting for something to explode, too. But he relaxed again when I went back to my stool and sat down.

Mom had said on the phone that the other women she was with now were loud, that she wasn't getting enough sleep. She probably wasn't eating very much, either. I closed my eyes, trying not to imagine how tired she probably looked now.

She needed me to come back to her so that she could go get help and start over. And I would be there. I wouldn't let her down. No matter what, I'd do what I had to do so that we could be together again. Everyone knew you had to make the most of things.

If you didn't, things had a way of making the most of you.

CHAPTER 23

A loud rap on the door made me jump. Toby barked twice and then ran over, sniffing at the space along the floor.

"Hello?" I held my breath as I slipped the rope back around his neck and leaned in close to the door. It had to be Margery. Maybe she'd forgotten something.

"Fred?"

I looked down at Toby, who barked again. It wasn't Margery. I unlocked the door and opened it a crack.

Lardvark gasped as she caught sight of Toby. "He's back! Where did you find him?"

"He found us." I wound the rope more tightly around my hand as Toby strained toward the opening. "Stay, Toby. No running, buddy. No jumping." But my mind wasn't really on Toby. Why was she here? Didn't she remember how we'd left things last night? How I'd gotten her in trouble?

"Holy cannoli." Lardvark stared at Toby curiously. "He looks so different. Did you guys give him a bath?"

"Yup. First the hose, then a real bath. Margery clipped his nails and gave him a haircut, too. Well, kind of. Mostly, she just trimmed everything."

"He looks so handsome." Lardvark sounded wistful. "Like a real dog."

"You hear that?" I grinned at Toby. "I bet you've never heard anyone call you handsome before."

"You guys did a great job," Lardvark said.

"Thanks." Why was she being so nice after I'd been so awful to her? "What are you doing here anyway? Isn't there school today?"

"Of course there's school." Lardvark leaned forward, trying to peer inside. "It's Thursday."

"Well, aren't you supposed to be there?"

"Yeah." She blinked and leaned in even farther. "But I skipped. Wow, this place looks really cool. Can I come in?"

"Um." I hesitated.

"Please? Just for a few minutes?"

"All right." I took a step back, sliding my fingers under the rope around Toby's neck. "Maybe for a few minutes. Hurry up, though, so he doesn't try to run."

Lardvark squeezed her way in and shut the door quickly. In her hands was a large brown paper bag.

Toby strained against the rope, but I held him tight. "Listen, I'm not in here just messing around," I told Lardvark. "Margery left me work to do. You know, because I got in trouble at school and everything. And

Toby's staying with me while I do it. It's not the greatest time for you to be here."

"I didn't sleep a wink last night." I wondered if Lardvark had even heard me, as she walked over and put the paper bag on the far end of the table. "I just stayed awake, thinking about you guys."

I led Toby back over to the table and reattached the rope to the leg. "You mean Toby?"

"Yeah. And you. I couldn't stop thinking about the day we had. It was crazy, you know? The whole thing. It was kind of nuts."

I couldn't disagree. Between getting suspended from school, finding Mr. Carder half-dead inside his house, Toby running off, Mom calling, and then Toby coming back, yesterday had been pretty wild.

"Have you heard anything about Mr. Carder?" Lardvark settled herself on one of the stools and picked up the candlestick. "He's still alive, right?"

"As far as I know." I took the candlestick out of her hand and put it back on the table. "You shouldn't touch stuff in here. It's Margery's." I was getting a little irritated. Sure, we'd had a few adventures yesterday. And yes, some of them had been intense. We'd even had a fight, which I guess we'd also made up from. But that didn't mean we were best friends now. Or that she could just come in here and act like she owned the place.

"Sorry." Lardvark hunched her shoulders at my words. That same hangdog expression she wore when she talked about Michelle came over her face. It made me crazy, seeing her like that.

"You don't have to be sorry," I said. "You didn't know."

Lardvark sat up straighter. "What is this place anyway? Like a workshop?"

"Yeah. Pretty much."

"So Margery, like, makes things?"

"Sort of." I shrugged, holding up the candlestick. "Although her idea of 'things' is a little bit different than most people's."

Lardvark squinted at the candlestick. "What's that going to be?"

"No idea." I rolled the candlestick between my hands. "She doesn't know yet, either. She says she waits till something tells her what it wants to be."

"Huh." Lardvark considered my statement. "That doesn't make any sense at all."

"Tell me about it." I put the candlestick back and plopped down beside her. "But you should see the stuff she comes up with."

"Like what?"

I told Lardvark about Margery's wheelbarrow chair and the kitchen table with the big silver wheels underneath. And I told her about the kitchen chairs with the mouse and the flower and vine carvings along the back. It was the strangest thing, telling her about them. Not because Lardvark and I weren't really friends. And not because I even cared what she thought about them all that much. It was more a feeling of admiration, listening to myself talk about Margery's stuff. Maybe even a little pride. Which I hadn't even known I felt until just that moment.

"Wow," Lardvark said. "That's really cool. I wish I could do something like that. I'm not good at anything."

"What about your unicycle?"

Lardvark shrugged. "My parents brought that back from Germany last year. I don't know why. I can barely ride a regular bike."

"But you can ride that," I said. "Can't you?"

She nodded, tracing an invisible line on the table. "Yeah. It took me a while, but I figured it out."

"That's pretty cool. Honestly, I don't know anyone who knows how to ride a unicycle."

Lardvark lifted her eyes. "That's because normal people don't have unicycles," she said softly. "They have bikes. With two wheels."

There was something about the way she said the word "normal" that made me sit up a little. And even though I had loads of work to do, and it meant leaving Toby inside for a few minutes without me, I heard myself say, "Who cares about being normal? I want to see you ride a unicycle."

"Right now?" Lardvark's eyebrow went up.

I nodded. "Yeah. Right now."

"Okay." Lardvark could hardly hide the smile on her face as she slid off the stool. "It's out front, on the porch. Come on."

CHAPTER 24

"You stay here, buddy." I rubbed the sides of Toby's neck. "We won't be long. Be a good boy, okay?"

He watched us as we slipped out, and I could hear him bark as the door closed behind us.

"He'll be okay, won't he?" Lardvark asked.

"Yeah. He can't go anywhere. I tied the rope to the table."

"You can tell he really likes you," Lardvark said. "He looks at you like you're his best friend in the whole world." She laughed a little bit. "If I wasn't so scared of him, I'd be jealous."

"You're still scared of him?" We were almost to the front of the house. I could see the unicycle seat leaning against the porch railing. It was red with black piping around the edge.

"I told you," Lardvark said. "All dogs make me nervous."

"Well, nervous and scared are two different things."

"Yeah." Lardvark sounded thoughtful. "Maybe."

The unicycle was bigger than I'd imagined, with a long seat and a thick wheel. But it looked kind of funny, too, the way something only half-there looks funny, and I found myself giggling as Lardvark brought it down from the porch.

"It's totally dorky, isn't it?" She held on to the seat with one hand and bounced the wheel up and down.

"No, no." I struggled to make my voice serious. "It's not dorky. I've just never seen one. You know, up close. It can't be easy to ride on one wheel."

"It wasn't at first." Lardvark rolled the wheel back and forth a few times, as if warming it up. "It took a lot of practice. I don't really have anything else to do, though, so it kind of worked out." She took the seat and put it between her legs. Two seconds later, she was on top of it, pedaling around the front yard, weaving around me, even going backward a few times. She held her arms out, and as the unicycle zoomed this way and that, she sat up straighter than I'd ever seen her before. Her blond bangs blew up along her forehead, and she held her lower lip with her teeth.

"Man!" I shouted as she whizzed around me a second time. "You're really good!"

"You think so?" Her cheeks flushed pink as she smiled. "Thanks. It's actually kind of fun when you get the hang of it."

"I can't believe you rode it here." I raised my voice a little as she pedaled farther down the driveway and back. "On the road and everything. What do people do when they see you? They must freak!"

Lardvark laughed. "They do. Some lady practically drove off the road, she was looking at me for so long. She almost smashed into a tree!"

"You can't really blame her." I shook my head. "It's not every day people see a girl riding a unicycle down the street."

She hopped off the seat in a single, fluid motion. The wheel spun a little as she held it out to me. "You want to sit on it? Just see how it feels?"

"Nah." I shook my head. "I'd be terrible. I've never even ridden a real bike. You know, with two wheels."

"You've never had a bike of your own?" Lardvark asked.

"Uh-uh." I could feel the heat rush to my face. There was no need to get into details about Mom not being able to afford one. "We used to live in the city. You know, Philadelphia. There wasn't any reason to get a bike. Too much traffic."

"Yeah." Lardvark was looking at me closely. Too closely. It made me uncomfortable. "Well, try it anyway. Maybe it's a good thing you've never ridden a real bike. You won't have anything to compare it to."

"I don't know."

"Oh, come on." She moved it closer to me, nudging my arm with the seat. "Aren't you even the littlest bit curious? Just sit on it. See how it feels. You can hold on to me the whole time. I'll make sure you don't fall."

I sighed deeply, like it was killing me to do it, or as if I was doing her a big favor, but the truth was, I was kind of curious to try it. Maybe even a little excited.

Lardvark took my hand as I positioned the seat between my legs and hoisted myself up. Almost immediately, the wheel spun out from under me. She grabbed me as I fell backward, and pulled me toward her. "Don't worry. I did that about six thousand times when I was first learning. Sit forward this time. Even if it feels really weird. Lean over from your waist and sit as far forward as you can. I'll hold you."

I tried again, and again the wheel slipped out from under me. "This is stupid," I said, shaking my head. "Seriously. I told you—I've never even sat on a real bike before."

"That doesn't—"

"It's fine." I held up my palms. "Really. I just wanted to see you ride it. Besides, I have to get back to work. But thanks for coming over. You know, and like checking up on me and everything."

Lardvark looked like I'd just punched her in the stomach. "Wait, you want me to go?"

"I have work to do. I told you before you could only stay a few minutes. I'm sorry. I don't mean to be rude."

"Yeah, okay. I understand." She blinked. "Can I at least say goodbye to Toby? I won't come in the shed. I'll just stand outside the door and wave to him."

I shrugged. "Sure."

It took us less than a minute to walk back around to the shed, but it was one of the most awkward moments of my life. With every step, I could feel Lardvark's disappointment getting heavier and heavier. I couldn't really blame her. She'd just skipped school and ridden her unicycle all the way over here to spend the day with me, and I'd told her she had to leave. But what choice did I have? I had to do the work Margery had left me. I just wished I didn't feel so terrible.

It was hard to tell whether I gasped first or screamed. Either way, both were loud and full of terror.

Because Toby was nowhere to be seen.

And Margery's workshop looked as if someone had taken a sledgehammer and smashed it to pieces.

CHAPTER 25

I didn't know where to look first. The worktable lay on its side, and the leg where Toby had been tied was completely torn off. Screws and bolts and doorknobs, wrenches and springs and even a few rusted pie tins, were scattered across the floor. Worst of all, though, was Margery's sculpture in the corner. The blue tarp had been torn off and the statue itself—whatever it was—had been knocked over. The clock in the middle was smashed to bits, and the large silver ladle was lying in a corner.

"Oh my God." I could barely get my voice out as I brought my hands to my mouth. "Ohmygodohmygod."

"Holy ravi*oli*." Lardvark glanced around nervously. "Do you think Toby did all of this? Where is he?"

I didn't answer her. Instead, I moved over to the table. "Help me with this, will you?" I lifted one side of it with two hands.

Lardvark hoisted the other end. The table was ridiculously heavy, but she was strong, and in a few minutes, we had it right side up again. It was wobbly minus the leg, but it was up. I glanced around the room, trying to figure out what to do next.

And then I saw something move under the blue tarp. I looked over at Lardvark, who was still holding one end of the table. "Can you hold it like that for a minute?" I eyed the blue tarp as it moved a second time. "I think I might know where the other leg to this table is."

I walked over to the corner, so angry I could have spit. Forget the work Margery had left for me to complete, and which for a second time I would not be able to finish. Forget even that Lardvark was here, uninvited again, probably without the permission of her parents. Now the rest of my day was going to be spent cleaning up this mess, thanks to one crazy dog. And it wasn't like it was going to take me a few extra minutes. I had to straighten things up so that it looked as though nothing had happened. It was going to take some serious effort. And time. I didn't know if I had either.

"Toby?"

A whining sound drifted out from under the tarp. "Toby, what did you do?" I lifted the tarp and stared at him. The rope was still around his neck, and at the other end, just as I'd thought, was the table leg. He had pulled and yanked and strained at that thing until the entire structure had given way. Despite the dreadfulness of the situation, I kind of had to hand it to him, too. It couldn't have been easy, taking something that big all the way down, especially since he was so small.

And then I noticed the big brown paper bag Lardvark had brought with her. It was torn to shreds, scattered around Toby like ragged postcards.

"What was in your bag?" I asked slowly.

"What?"

"Your bag." I turned around, glaring at Lardvark. "What was in it?"

"Oh no." Lardvark's face fell as the table sagged in her hands.

I leaned down and picked up a torn scrap of the bag. "What was in it?"

"Salami," Lardvark whimpered. "And German bologna. To give to Margery. You know, because we took hers last night without asking."

I blinked. "And you left a bag full of meat five feet away from a tied-up dog while we went out and got on your stupid *unicycle*?" I hadn't meant for my voice to get louder, but by the time I said the word "unicycle," I was shouting. "How could you be so dumb?"

Lardvark watched me fearfully, her blue eyes filling with tears. "I—I . . ." she stammered, shaking her head.

"HOW?" I yelled.

Tears spilled out of Lardvark's eyes. "I don't know," she sobbed. "I just am."

For some reason, her response made me even angrier. "Give me a real answer!" I pushed my face in close as I yelled. "Say something! *Do* something!"

"I can't!" she whimpered.

"Yes, you can! Stop being such a wimp all the time and stand up for yourself!" I had the sensation of being outside my body, the way I had when I went flying over the table toward Michelle. It wasn't me, talking in such a terrible way to Lardvark. It couldn't be. "The only reason people push you around is because you let them, you know that? Because you're too much of a baby to tell them to knock it off!" I could hear Toby barking in the background, like he was telling me to stop.

"Why are you doing this?" Lardvark was sobbing now, her pale, doughy face streaked with tears. "I thought you were different from everyone at school! I thought you were nice!"

I could feel my breath pushing in and out of my nose as I stared at her. When *had* I turned into one of those terrible girls at school? And why was I acting like a crazy person toward someone who wanted to be my friend? "I am nice," I muttered.

Lardvark made a whimpering sound. "I . . . I didn't think about the bag. I was just so excited to show you the unicycle . . ." Her voice trailed off.

I lifted my eyes to meet hers. My heart slowed inside my chest. "It was an accident. I shouldn't have yelled at you like that. I'm sorry."

"It's okay." Lardvark dabbed at her eyes. "I'm kind of used to it."

"You shouldn't be used to it." I pushed down a small knob of frustration. "You have to stand up for yourself. Especially with people like Michelle."

Lardvark took a deep, shaky breath. "I know," she said. "But what if I did get in Michelle's face, and she hauled off and knocked me on my butt? Then what?"

"Then you stand back up and do it again. People aren't going to keep knocking you down if you keep getting back up."

Lardvark sighed. "You make it sound easy, but it's not."

"I know." I almost reached out then and touched her hand. Almost. "But you've got to start somewhere. You've got to at least try."

She stared at the floor for a moment and then looked up again. "Please let me stay and help you clean up. It'll go twice as fast if both of us do it."

She had me there. Two pairs of hands would get a lot more work done than one. "Okay." It took some time, but the two of us managed to shove the leg back in place and hammer it steady. When we were finished, it looked pretty good. Now we just had to get the rest of the place together before Margery got home.

"Hey," I said, hanging the hammer back on the wall. "What would you think if I called you Delia from now on? You know, instead of Ardelia?"

Lardvark stared at me.

"Just as a nickname," I said. "If you don't like it, I'll—"

"I love it," Delia interrupted. "It's just . . . no one's ever called me that before. It's been Lardvark for so long at school, and Ardelia at home . . ." Her voice drifted off.

"Well, it'll be Delia here," I said. "At least for me and Toby."

She smiled at me then, and her lower lip quivered. I thought about how Toby had nuzzled into the front of me this morning after I'd taken his leash off, and I wondered if this was Delia's way of saying thank you.

Once the table was done, I could feel myself start to breathe a little easier. Except for Margery's mangled sculpture in the corner, things were starting to feel a bit more manageable. And if we did a good enough job, maybe Margery would never know anything had happened at all.

We knelt on the floor and began sorting screws and nuts and bolts into individually marked coffee cans. For a few long minutes, we worked in silence.

"Can I ask you a question?" Delia asked suddenly. "Do you miss Philadelphia? It's such a cool city. It's so boring out here."

"Things aren't all that cool in the city." I scooped my pile of bolts into my hand and poured them into the coffee can. "And I'm just here for a little while."

"Oh yeah?" I could hear the disappointment in her voice. "Like, how long?"

"Just a few more weeks, I think." I moved the can to the top of the table and started in on the screws.

"And then you go back to Philadelphia again?"

"Maybe. My mom's been talking about going somewhere new. Getting a fresh start."

"From what?"

"What do you mean?"

"You said she wants to get a fresh start." Delia was still hunched over on her knees, sorting through her bolts. "Why?"

I could feel myself bristle. My life was none of her business. And even if it was (which it wasn't), why did she need to know? "Not really sure," I mumbled. "Just a thing she wants to do."

Delia nodded. "We moved here to get a fresh start," she said. "Well, my parents did. I was only five. I was just kind of along for the ride."

"What was their fresh start from?" I asked, thinking she might say something like they needed a change of scenery or wanted to build a bigger house. Anyone whose parents went to Germany and brought back a unicycle for their kid had to have money.

Instead, Delia said, "I had an older brother who drowned. Back when we lived in Ohio. He was fooling around with our dog, Sampson, and they both fell into the pool. My mom and dad didn't talk for a whole year after it happened. Not to me, not to each other, not to anyone. And then one day, they told me we were moving." She shrugged. "We came here. I think it was supposed to be their fresh start. My dad bought the iron company. And my mom just keeps decorating the house. But they still don't talk." She paused. "I think they tried. To do the fresh start thing. But . . ." Her voice trailed off. "Well, you know."

"It's pretty quiet in your house, then, huh?"

Delia shot me a look, as if she wasn't quite sure if I was making fun of her situation.

"No, really," I said hurriedly. "It's got to be awful." I wondered if the silence in that house was anything like the silence in the apartment in Philadelphia. Did Delia know what that kind of silence felt like?

"It's worse than awful," she said quietly. "Because they're there, you know? They're *right* there—" She choked on the last word and inhaled quickly. "And they still won't talk to me. You know, except for the basics. Hi, bye, excuse me. That kind of thing. It's like I don't exist."

All of a sudden, I felt as though I could see Delia. Like, *really* see her. Up until that moment, it was as if I'd kind of been talking and listening to her from behind a curtain. And just then, totally without warning, the curtain slid to one side and I could see her standing there for real. She wasn't just the sad, cream-puffy person I'd thought she was. She was someone completely different. Someone even a little bit like me.

This time, I did put my hand on Delia's arm. "You do exist," I told her. "Okay? And you totally, one hundred percent should be here."

Her whole face relaxed. "That might be the nicest thing anyone's ever said to me," she said softly.

"Well, it's true." I let go of her arm and went back to work. For a few minutes, the only sound in the room was the clink and ping of the bolts dropping into the can.

"The same goes for you, you know," Delia said. "You exist, too, Fred. And you should be here."

I didn't answer right away, and let my fingers linger among the pile of screws I was sorting. I knew Delia was trying to make me feel good, but her words felt . . . strange. Untrue. I didn't belong here, and no matter what she said, I never would.

CHAPTER 26

It was almost noon by the time we got everything sorted again and put back in place. The workshop looked as good as new, or at least as good as it could again after being torn apart.

"Wow," Delia said, putting her hands on her hips. "Margery will never know anything happened."

I walked over to the sculpture in the corner. "Except for this." We had picked it up off the floor and set it back on its stand, but it was still horribly mangled. I reached out and fingered something dangling from the middle of it. I wasn't completely sure, but it looked like part of a watch. Or at least the wristband section. "I don't even know where to start when it comes to this."

"What *is* it?" Delia cocked her head, looking at it.

"I'm not sure. It must be something Margery's been working on." I sighed. "She's going to freak."

"Why does she have to see it? Let's just cover it up

again," Delia said. "Maybe we can fix it over the next few days while she's gone. She'll never even know what happened."

"What do you mean, *we* can fix it?" I asked. "Delia, you have to go to school. You're going to get in trouble."

"With who?" She lifted her chin a little. "My parents? They don't care what I do as long as I stay out of their way. Trust me."

"The school'll call them," I argued. "They'll tell them you're skipping. And then—"

"And then what?" She looked at me defiantly. "You think that hasn't happened already?"

"You've skipped school before?"

"Would you want to go to a place every day where people called you Lardvark?" Her blue eyes flashed. "Or where you sit at a desk and wait for the most popular girl in school to tap you on the shoulder just to let you know she's more important than you?"

I dropped my eyes.

"You only have one more day of being suspended," Delia said. "It's not like I'm going to skip for a whole week or anything. Just let me come again tomorrow. We can work on this thing." She nodded toward Margery's sculpture. "And see how much we can get done. Together."

"You could be a lawyer, you know that?" I grinned at her. "You're really good at arguing."

"That's a good thing, right?" Delia looked embarrassed again.

"Yeah." I nodded. "That's a really good thing."

I half expected to see the back steps torn out as Delia and I returned to the workshop after lunch, but Toby was just sitting there quietly. He barked as we rounded the corner, and strained on his rope.

"He really is sweet," Delia said, watching as I rubbed him around his neck and buried my nose in his clean fur. "You'd think an animal that had been treated so badly would just be mean and horrible." She shrugged. "I know I would be."

I thought about Delia's situation and how, in some ways, she'd been treated a little bit like Toby, with the most important people in her life barely acknowledging her. "No, you wouldn't," I said, untying the leash from the post.

"You don't think so?" She held the door open as Toby bounded inside again.

"Nope." I shut the door behind us and locked it.

"That's nice of you to say."

"I'm not trying to be nice. I'm telling you the truth."

"But why do you think that?" Delia's face was so hopeful that it made the back of my throat hurt.

I shrugged. "You're tough, Delia. You've been through

a lot, first with your family, then with all those jerks at school. And you still get up every day and do your thing." I picked up the candlestick and started on it with the sander. "I think that's strong."

She picked at the skin along one thumb. "I'm pretty wimpy with those kids at school, though."

My face flushed as I thought of how terrible I'd been to her earlier. "Not too many people would know how to deal with something like that."

"How would you deal with it?"

"I'm not really sure. All situations are different."

"But if you were me," she pressed, "and Michelle Palmer never ever let you alone, what would you do? And please don't say that you would tell a teacher or another adult, because you know that only makes things a thousand times worse."

Delia was looking at me steadily. It was a little nerve-racking, mostly because I didn't want to let her down. But I also didn't want to steer her in the wrong direction. "I'd have to face Michelle," I said finally. "I can't think of any other way someone like that would stop. You'd have to be tough. Really tough. Let her know that you're finished. That you won't take it anymore."

"But *how*?"

I could hear the whimper in her question, and something inside me flared. "By not sounding like that, for starters."

"Like what?" Still with the whimper.

I put the candlestick down. "You can't sound like you're begging when you tell someone you're done being their doormat. You can't *ask*. You have to put your foot down, Delia. You have to say, 'No. More.'"

She looked at her shoes for what seemed like a long time. Then she lifted her head. "I don't know if I can do that."

"I think you can," I said. "Actually, I know you can. You have to practice. Just like anything else. Try it. See how it feels."

"Right now?"

"Yeah, why not?" I put my sander down. "Pretend you're in science class, and I'm Michelle, and I'm coming over to tap you on the shoulder."

"All right." Delia rolled her eyes as she turned around. "This feels really weird."

"I know." I made my way over to the door. "Just try it anyway. Close your eyes, maybe. Try to really imagine that I'm her."

Delia took a deep breath and let it out again. "Okay. I'm ready."

Toby had stopped poking around and was standing there, watching us. It was sort of like he knew that we were doing something serious, and he had to be still for it.

I opened and shut the door to give Delia a signal. Then I walked over and tapped her on the shoulder. She turned her head and looked at me. "Please don't do that anymore," she whispered.

"Nope." I shook my head. "You can't use the word 'please.' And raise your voice. You gotta sound like you really mean it, Delia. Try it again."

I went back over to the door. Open. Shut. I walked across the floor and tapped her on the shoulder. Delia hunched her shoulders at my touch and stared at the table. "Don't do that anymore."

"Better!" I clapped my hands. "It's so much better without 'please' in it! Okay, this time sit up straighter and try to say it a little bit louder. And look at me when you do it. Right in the eyes, like you're not afraid."

"I think I'm good for today," Delia said. "But thanks."

"Wait, what?" I knuckled her gently in the shoulder. "Come on, we're just getting started!"

"I know." Delia hung her head. "I just don't want to do any more right now."

I looked at her for a minute without saying anything. A big part of me wanted to push her, to tell her that the worst thing she could do right now was quit. But then I thought about how I'd felt on the unicycle. It was embarrassing, being so unskilled at something. Especially in front of someone else.

"Okay. We can try again another time." I nodded at the small wheel on the table in front of her. "You want to sand that? If you help, we can get these three things finished in half the time. Then we'll go look at the sculpture in the corner."

"All right." Delia took the sander and settled herself on one of the stools. She looked relieved and maybe a little bit grateful. "Thanks, Fred."

"For what?"

"For, you know, wanting to help me." Delia's cheeks flushed.

"Sure," I said. "It's no big deal."

She gave me a look, and I knew what I'd just said wasn't true. At least not for her. It was a big deal. Maybe the biggest deal she'd encountered in a long, long time.

I was about halfway through my candlestick when Delia asked me what my favorite subject in school was.

"Science," I said, without hesitation.

She wrinkled her nose. "Ugh, really? I think science is one of the most boring things on the planet."

I snorted. "Science is a lot of things, Delia, but boring isn't one of them."

"I always fall asleep in class."

"That's too bad," I said. "You're missing out."

"On what?"

"On everything! Like, you just mentioned planets. Did you know that Earth is the fifth-largest planet in the solar system? And that seventy percent of it is water?"

"No." Delia shook her head. "I didn't know that."

"How about bones? You know anything about bones?"

"Like our bones?"

"Any bones," I answered. "How about this? What's the only animal on the planet with hollow ones?"

"No idea."

"*Birds!*" I grinned. "How else do you think they'd get off the ground?"

"Huh." Delia looked at me curiously for a moment. "You know, you should think about joining the Middle School Quiz Bowl at school. You could compete in the science category."

"What's the Quiz Bowl?"

"Oh my gosh, it's a huge deal. Everyone comes, even parents. There's a trophy for the winning team and everything. They hold it every year, right before Christmas break."

"But what *is* it?"

"It's a huge quiz game for the middle school kids. All the questions are about science and math. There's two teams and twelve rounds. Sometimes at the end of twelve rounds, the game gets tied, and it has to go to a lightning round. That's what happened last year. The kids get really competitive, too. Probably because you have to try out for it to even get on a team."

"How do you try out?"

"You have to take a test. Before Thanksgiving, I think. The three highest scorers in each subject get to play in the bowl. I've never done it before, but I think I'm going to take the one for math this year. I'm pretty good at math."

Delia's eyes practically glittered as she spoke, and I could feel her excitement. It was weird, but I don't think I realized how disappointed I'd been when I was called out of Mr. Poole's Science Jeopardy game until just that moment. Coming so close to winning a class competition had been tough. Especially when I knew I was *thisclose* to taking the whole thing.

"I don't know," I said. "It doesn't really sound like my thing."

"Why not?" Delia rubbed her sander harder across her wheel. "You know that stuff you just told me about Earth and birds and stuff? Those are the exact kind of questions they ask in the bowl. You'd be perfect, Fred. I'm telling you. They'd love to have you on the team. Just think about it, okay?"

"Okay," I answered, knowing perfectly well that I wouldn't. For starters, there was no way I was even going to be here to take the test or compete in the bowl.

And I didn't really care about any of that stuff right now anyway. There were bigger—and much more important—things I had to worry about.

Of course, Delia didn't have to know any of that.

And I had no plans to tell her.

CHAPTER 27

Delia's wheel was much smoother and cleaner than mine by the time we finished, and I might have been a little bit jealous if I wasn't so relieved. Now I'd be able to show Margery that I'd actually done what she'd asked me to do and hadn't just been messing around. It was almost four when we wiped the table down and set the sanded items on a clean cloth for Margery to inspect.

"Don't take this the wrong way," I said as we headed over to the corner to look at the sculpture, "but you should probably go. After last night . . ."

Delia's face fell. "I know. I was thinking about that. Margery probably never wants to see me again after I lied to her."

"No, it's not that. It's just . . . she got real nervous when she realized your parents didn't know you were here. I guess she just doesn't want to be responsible if something happens. She's got enough on her plate right now, taking care of me."

I closed my mouth quickly. I'd gone and done it again. Blurted out something totally personal without even thinking about it. I braced myself, waiting for Delia to ask me what I meant, why Margery was even taking care of me at all. But she didn't.

"Yeah, okay," she said instead. "What if I left, though, and then came back? If you wanted me to, I mean. I could just have my mom drop me off. She wouldn't care. And then Margery would know for sure that my parents were okay with it."

"That might work." I shrugged. "You want to come back? Like for dinner or something?"

"YES!" Delia practically shouted.

I laughed. "Okay. Stay here for a minute. I'll go in and call Margery and ask her."

"You think she'll say no?" Delia winced.

"I doubt it." I threw my coat on over my shoulders. "She likes you."

"She does?"

"Oh yeah." I yanked open the door. "She told me last night that you were a cool cat."

"She said that?" Delia's eyes got big. "Seriously?"

"Seriously." I nodded at Toby and scruffed him under the ears. "You be a good boy now. Don't jump on Delia. I'll be right back."

I could hear the phone ringing from the front porch. "All right, all right, I'm coming." I shut the door behind me and trotted into the kitchen. It was probably Margery, checking in to see how everything was going. I grabbed the receiver as it rang a final time and pressed it to my ear.

"Everything is totally fine," I said, sinking down into one of the metal chairs. "And Toby is behaving much better, too."

"Um, hello?" It wasn't Margery.

"Oh." I sat up straight. "I'm sorry. Hello?"

"Fred?"

"Yeah?"

"Hi, honey! It's Carmella, from Children and Youth Services! How are you?"

I stood up quickly and walked over to the window. "I'm fine. Is something wrong?"

"No, no," Carmella said. "I'm just calling to see how things are going."

"Oh." I took a deep breath. "Okay."

"How's Margery? You two getting along?"

"Sure."

"Great." A pause. "Well, I wanted to touch base with you about a few things. Your mom's hearing will take place in about three weeks. And from what we've heard, she's planning to cooperate."

"Which means what?"

"If she admits to what she did, she'll get to go home. Telling the truth, combined with the fact that she will have already spent time in jail, will probably mean she only gets something like probation." Carmella paused. "And it'll give her the chance to bring you home."

My head nodded up and down like a jack-in-the-box. So far everything Mom had told me was adding up, except the part where she'd have to say she was guilty of stealing. It wasn't like Mom to lie about anything, but if that was what she had to do in order to "cooperate" and get me back, I guessed it wasn't a big deal. It was only a little white lie anyway.

"They won't give her a hard time, will they?" I asked. "I mean, about me going back to live with her?"

"There will be a dependency hearing for that," Carmella said. "We'll all have to be there: me, you, Margery, and your mom. It won't be in an actual court-room or anything. But there will be a judge. And we'll all have to tell him what's been going on and how your mom is doing now. Then he'll make a decision about whether or not you can go live with her again."

"Wait, there's a chance she won't get me back? How can that be?" I stood up straighter, my spine as rigid as a pole.

"Oh, Fred, honey. It depends on what the judge sees and hears from us. Especially from you. He'll want to make sure you're being taken care of. Can you under-stand that?"

I didn't answer. I didn't care about any judge. I didn't care who he was or how important a job he held, or even that he had the power to keep Mom and me apart. I was as strong as he was. And if Mom was going to have to tell a little white lie to get back to me, I'd do the same thing. As long as we weren't lying to each other, nothing else mattered. I'd already promised her that I'd do whatever it took to make sure we stayed together. And I would. I'd go in there and paint the prettiest picture possible— so pretty that even Carmella would shake her head and wonder why we'd ever been separated in the first place.

"Fred?" Carmella said. "Are you still there?"

"Yeah. Is that everything?"

"That's everything," Carmella said. "Unless there's anything you want to talk about some more?"

"No."

"Okay, then. It was good to touch base again, honey. You take care of yourself, you hear? I'll call back next week to see how things are going."

"Okay."

"See you, Fred."

"See you."

I hung up the phone and stood there for a long time without moving. The tree branches in Mr. Carder's yard made shadows on the kitchen wall, their long, spindly arms and fingers swaying back and forth like a ghost waving goodbye.

I stood very still, watching them reach farther and farther as the sun began to set. When they faded again into nothing, I walked out of the house.

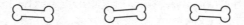

I couldn't remember anymore why I'd grabbed Mom's jean jacket to wear that day, but I did recall putting my hand inside the front pocket, feeling a small bottle, and pulling it out. I could see through the orange plastic that there weren't any pills inside, but that didn't stop the panicky feeling from spreading across my chest. More and more, I'd been spotting empty bottles around the apartment: on Mom's night table, wedged into the medicine cabinet, in the door of the fridge.

"Fr—" Mom stopped cold as she came out of the bathroom, a hairbrush in her hands. Her eyes darted to the bottle and then up to me again, quick as lightning. Panic flashed across her face and then disappeared again. "Put that back, honey."

I held her eyes as I slid the bottle back into the pocket of her jacket. "Another one?"

She reached up and started brushing her hair again. "It's just Gwyneth's, from work. She gave it to me so I could refill her prescription while she's away on vacation." She didn't look at me as she talked. Electric static crackled through the brush. Her face was as pale as cotton.

"Mom."

She kept brushing. "What?"

"It's really Gwyneth's?"

"Yes!" Still no eye contact. "Look at the label."

She was right. The label did have Gwyneth's name on it. But the date said the prescription was a year old. "The label doesn't mean anything."

"Of course it does!" Mom's eyes darted across the floor. "It means it belongs to Gwyneth."

"You swear?" I hesitated. "To the moon and back?"

The brush paused halfway down—so quickly that if I hadn't been watching her so closely, I would have missed it. "Yes," she said. "Now come on, honey. We've gotta go. If I'm late for work again today, Mr. McCormick will make my life more of a nightmare than it already is."

We walked the three blocks together holding hands the way we always did, and when we turned off Broad Street, Mom started singing one of my favorite songs, but something was off, and I could feel it, deep in my bones, where I kept things to myself. I knew what empty bottles meant. And I knew what outdated prescriptions meant, too. Still, I tried to convince myself otherwise. Mom had never lied when I'd asked her to swear on something. And swearing to the moon and back was serious business, something neither of us took lightly. It was a promise to tell the truth no matter what. No matter how hard.

It was the first time in my life that I didn't believe her.

"She said no."

Delia's face fell as I gave her the news. She put her phone on the table and stared at me. I waited to feel bad for disappointing her, or even to feel guilty about lying, but I didn't feel either one. I didn't feel anything at all. I just wanted to be alone.

"She did?" Delia's whimper was back. "Really? How come?"

I shrugged, pretending to busy myself with the sculpture in the corner. "She just said it wasn't a good night. We have a lot going on."

"Like what?"

"I don't know, Delia. That's just what she said." I didn't mean to sound impatient, but the look on Delia's face told me I wasn't doing a very good job. "I'm sorry. Another time, though, okay?"

"Yeah, okay." Delia looked back down at her phone and tapped the screen. "So I was looking at the school's website while you were gone, and there's like five or six pages of sample questions for the Quiz Bowl that I thought . . ."

But I wasn't listening. "Actually, you should probably just leave right now. Margery's coming home early. If she catches you here again, we're both going to be in trouble."

"Oh." Delia withdrew her hand slowly. "Okay." She shoved her phone into her back pocket and looked down at the floor. "Well, I guess I'll see you around, then."

"Yeah." I couldn't look at her as she walked across the room and put on her coat. And I only nodded when she said goodbye. But when I heard the door open and close behind her, I squeezed my eyes shut so tightly that I saw little pinpoints of light behind my lids. They zoomed this way and that way and then . . .

"Fred?"

My eyes flew open. I hadn't even heard the doorknob turn. "Yeah?"

"Did I do something?"

"No."

"Are you sure?" Delia's head poked through the door. Her eyebrows were raised like sideways parentheses. "You can tell me if I did. I'd rather know."

"You didn't."

"You're positive?"

"YES!" I turned on her then. "JUST GO, ALL RIGHT?"

She shut the door quickly. This time, it stayed closed.

The sculpture loomed in front of me like something wounded. Something beautiful and ugly and so deeply hurt that just then, looking at it again, I knew there was no possibility of ever putting it back together. Delia and I were kidding ourselves to think we could do anything that would make a difference, especially in a day or two. There was just no way.

My eyes searched the tools on the wall behind it until they fell on a large wrench. It was at least as long as my arm, maybe even longer. I took it down off the hook. It was heavy. I had to hold it carefully with both hands.

And then I smashed it against Margery's sculpture. Once and then again and again and again until the very last spring fell to the floor, bounced and skittered into a corner, and rolled to a stop.

CHAPTER 28

I was out front, holding Toby by his leash, when Margery pulled up on her motorcycle. I knew I couldn't prevent her from going into the workshop at some point, but I planned to stall her as long as I could. It wasn't quite dark yet, and the stretch of sky overhead was the color of a bruise. Toby barked when he saw Margery and kept barking as she parked the bike and turned off the engine.

"Hey there!" Margery grinned broadly as she took off her helmet and hung it on the handle of the bike. "How's things?"

"Pretty good." I leaned forward as Toby strained toward Margery, instead of pulling back on the rope. I'd figured out he didn't fight as hard when I did that, and it saved my arm from being yanked out of the socket. "You get that leash for Toby?"

"You bet I did." Margery opened a sack on the back of the bike and pulled out a bright blue cord. "This one has a soft collar, too, so it won't bite into his neck." She came over and showed me. "This loop attaches to the clothesline so he can run back and forth and up and down without anything yanking at him. It's just temporary." She bent down and scruffed Toby around the neck. "How does that sound, little guy? Huh?"

She led Toby over to the clothesline and clipped the leash to it. We both stood there for a moment, watching him race up and down the length of the yard. Despite my nerves, I couldn't help but smile. He looked so happy.

"What do you mean, it's just temporary?" I asked.

"We'll just use this until we can train him to come back when we call him. Then we can really let him run." Margery jerked her chin toward the house. "Let's go inside. I'm starving. After we eat, you can show me what you did in the shop."

I followed her into the house, trying hard to push down my rising panic. Still, I knew there was no getting around it. She was going to find out what I'd done to her sculpture. It was only a matter of time. I just couldn't imagine what would come next. Carmella would definitely be called; that was a given. I'd probably be sent back, placed with some other family. Maybe Margery would even press charges; after all, I'd destroyed her personal property for no good reason. People called the police about stuff like that, didn't they?

". . . and he really did break his neck." I snapped to

attention as Margery mentioned Mr. Carder. "Or at least a vertebra inside his neck. It broke from his fall down the steps. They're not sure if he'll ever walk again."

I knew there were thirty-three bones in the spine and that six or seven of them were in the neck. I wondered which one of Mr. Carder's had broken. "Is he in a cast?"

"More of a head brace." Margery made hand motions around her head to show me. "It's like a huge open cube with rods in it. All the rods are holding his head and neck in place so that they can heal."

I shuddered, thinking of it. "Is he still unconscious?"

"No." Margery peeled back the plastic on a package of ground meat. "We actually had a conversation. Maybe the first real conversation I've had with the man in twenty-seven years."

"He can talk?"

Margery nodded. "Watch me first." She took a chunk of the meat, rolled it between her palms until it formed a ball, and then pressed it lightly between the heels of her hands until a patty formed. "Okay?"

"Got it." I took the package as Margery slid it over to me.

"Oh, he talked all right," Margery said. "Mostly about you."

My hands froze around a wad of meat. "Me?"

"You and Ardelia. He said you guys saved his life. That if you hadn't been near the fence or heard him calling, he would have died there on that floor. All alone."

I could feel Margery watching me, but I couldn't look at her. Not yet. "I'm sure someone would've found him. Eventually."

"Who?" Margery washed her hands, then reached inside a drawer and pulled out a knife. "Who would've found him? He doesn't talk to anyone. He doesn't have any friends, as far as I can see. Heck, his only son still hadn't been to the hospital when I dropped by. No one would've heard him, Fred. You did that."

"Delia's the one who heard him, actually." I concentrated hard on shaping the meat into a patty. It was cold and squishy. "She's the one who should get the credit."

"Delia?" Margery asked.

Something lurched in my chest as I realized my mistake. "Yeah, you know, Ardelia."

"That's what she likes to be called? Delia?"

I nodded.

"Well, you're both heroes in my book." Margery began peeling an onion. "Delia for hearing him in the first place, and you for staying with him like you did until the ambulance got there." She paused. "He told me that, you know. That you stayed there with him until help arrived."

"Yeah." I nodded again without turning around.

"That meant more to him than anything." I could hear Margery walking toward me, and I hunched my shoulders, as if the motion might make her stop. It was agonizing, sitting and listening to her go on about me like I was some kind of superwoman while the shattered remains of her sculpture lay less than one hundred feet behind us. Margery stopped when she reached the table and pressed her hands down flat against it. "Look at me, Fred."

I bit my lip and raised my eyes.

"Mr. Carder thought he was going to die." She spoke slowly, wanting me to absorb her words. "Literally. He said he felt as though he was passing from one world into the next as he lay there, just drifting, sort of, between the two of them. He wasn't too clear about the other place, but he said that it was you, Fred, *you*, who he held on to in this one." She paused, her eyes squinting at the corners. "It's a big thing, what you did, whether you realize it or not."

The way she was looking at me was so intense I couldn't do anything but blink. Margery smiled a little and nodded, almost as if she was encouraging me to say something.

Anything.

"I did something terrible today," I whispered.

CHAPTER 29

Margery stood very still for a moment, looking down at her smashed sculpture. I stood all the way across the room, behind the table, and waited. My face burned with shame, and I could hear my heart banging around in my chest like a tennis ball. She stooped down and picked something up. Fingered it in her hand for a moment. "And you did this why?"

I didn't have an answer. The real one, which started with Toby wrecking the place and ended with me thinking about Mom, was too complicated. I still wasn't sure it was a real answer anyway. "I don't know." My voice was a whisper.

Margery stood back up. She tossed her long braid over her shoulder and turned around. "'I don't know' is not an answer, Fred."

I stared down at the table. My insides felt like Jell-O.

"I want an answer," Margery said. "And we're not

leaving here until you give me one." She set the piece on the table and waited.

The silence was unbearable. Maybe even worse than the silence in the apartment with Mom. My brain raced this way and that as I tried to decide where to start. How much to say. How much to leave out.

"Just tell me what happened." Margery settled herself on a stool and hiked one leg over the other. She wasn't going anywhere. "Stop trying to figure out what version of the story you think will make me the least angry and just tell me the truth."

I glanced over at her, wondering if she could read my mind.

"I was your age once, too." Margery raised her eyebrows and tapped the side of her head. "I remember how it works in there."

I told her all of it, even the part where I'd gotten so furious at Delia for leaving the paper bag behind and then later, when we'd practiced her standing up to Michelle Palmer. I told her about Carmella calling and the hearing that she and Mom and me would all have to go to in a few weeks so that Mom could get me back. I told her how, after that, I'd returned to the shop and told Delia she had to go home. And that after Delia had left, I'd thought about Mom in the apartment in Philadelphia, which had made me so angry that I took a wrench and smashed the sculpture to bits. When I finished, I hung my head and stared at the floor. I was exhausted.

Margery hadn't said a word during the whole thing, not even to ask a question. Now she uncrossed her legs. Folded her hands. "And that's everything?" she asked.

I nodded, but it wasn't the truth. I'd left out the part about why thinking about Mom had made me so upset. And of course no one knew what Mom had asked me to do when she'd called. No one would ever know that.

"This isn't going to come as any surprise to you," Margery said, watching me steadily, "but you are one angry girl."

I looked down at the floor.

"I'm not telling you that to embarrass you," she continued. "Being angry isn't a bad thing. And it doesn't make you a bad person." She paused. "I'm speaking from experience. I know what it's like to be that ticked off. It's horrible because the anger runs so deep and hurts so bad. Sometimes it almost feels like an actual, living thing inside you. An animal, maybe."

I didn't dare look up. My eyes were glued to the floor as I concentrated on breathing in and out. I felt transparent, as if Margery could see all the way inside me.

"You have two options here, Fred. You can feed that living thing and help it grow into something so big that you beat up everyone at Conestoga Middle School and destroy the rest of my personal property. Or you can starve it by putting all that energy into something else. Something better. The way I did."

I flicked my eyes up. "What'd you do?"

Margery jerked her head toward the statue. "I started working with junk. Finding it, cleaning it up, making stuff out of it."

"How'd that help?"

"I'm not sure, exactly." Margery hooked her thumbs through the belt loops on her jeans. "Taking things people had thrown to the curb and turning them into something beautiful just made me feel good." She shrugged. "It quieted that animal inside."

I wanted to ask her what kind of animal she had inside—and why—but I couldn't bring myself to do it. Those were big, scary questions. I wasn't sure I wanted to know the answers. "I'm sorry about your sculpture," I said instead. "I'd do anything to take it back."

Margery watched me for a long time without saying anything. "You don't have to take it back," she said finally. "But you do have to rebuild it."

"Rebuild it?" I echoed. "But I don't know what you want it to be."

"I don't want it to be anything," Margery said. "Except what you decide to make it. I want you to start from the beginning and build something all your own. And I want you to do it before you go back to Philadelphia."

I stared at Margery, wondering if she was kidding.

"I don't know how to do that," I said finally.

"You'll figure it out." She stood up. "And if you're angry that I'm making you do this, that's okay. When you learn how to use the anger inside you to create instead of destroy, you'll realize it's one of the greatest tools you'll ever have."

I had no idea what she was talking about, but I didn't want to tell her that and risk listening to some twenty-minute explanation about feelings. "Okay," I said instead, shaking my head.

"Think of it as your punishment," Margery said. "Which, considering the crime, is a very generous one in my book. Now, let's go back inside and eat. I don't know if you remember what I told you about me when I get hungry, but it ain't pretty."

CHAPTER 30

We didn't talk much during dinner. I think we were both drained from the talk in the shop, and there wasn't really all that much to say after that anyway. We worked with Toby, though, after we cleaned up, letting him off his leash and bringing him back inside the shop.

"You get a chance at all to do the paw press?" Margery asked as Toby jumped up on her.

"Yeah." I watched as she grabbed his paws in both hands and squeezed, all the while telling him no. Toby dropped back down immediately and whined. "I'm not as good at it as you, though. He keeps jumping up on me."

"He'll keep doing that until it clicks." Margery squatted down and patted Toby on the head. "That's how it works with animals. You've got to be consistent. Do the same thing, over and over and over again. That's the only way they learn."

I told her about Delia's brother then, about how their dog, Sampson, had drowned him by accident.

Margery shook her head. "That was an untrained dog," she said grimly. "And he probably thought the boy was in danger, which is why he jumped in after him. What a tragedy."

I thought about telling her the rest of the story, too, how Delia's parents had stopped talking afterward, and how they still didn't talk, not even to her, which made her feel like she didn't belong here. That she hadn't ever been meant to be here. But I didn't. That was between Delia and me. And for some reason, even though I was unsure where things between Delia and me stood, I wanted to keep it that way.

"Let's start with sit," Margery said, standing back up. She reached into the front pocket of her jeans, pulled out a kibble, and held it by her side. "Sit, Toby!" She followed the command by slicing her arm up and lifting the kibble toward her shoulder. Toby peered up at her with his big eyes. "Sit!" she said again, repeating the hand motion. Toby whined. "Sit!" Margery repeated the command, along with the hand slice, at least ten more times until, suddenly, without warning, Toby lowered his haunches and sat down.

"Oh, man!" I clapped my hands. "He did it!"

"Of course he did it. He's a very, very smart boy. And now he gets a reward." She held the kibble out to Toby and grinned as he snapped it up. "You should always reward them when they do what you ask. Never punish. Always, always reward."

She stroked his black-and-white fur with her thick hand and cooed a bit more at him. And when she did that, I got the feeling that I'd had earlier with Delia and the curtain. It wasn't as dramatic; Margery was only pulling back a little part of her curtain. But it was a real part. A true part. And it made me happy, seeing it.

Maybe, I thought later, there were more sides to Margery I hadn't seen yet.

Maybe everyone hid pieces of themselves until it was safe to bring them out and show them to someone else.

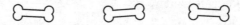

"Who taught you how to do all that?" I asked later, after we'd settled Toby in his little bed and gone back into the kitchen. Margery was sipping her tea, and I was drinking a glass of milk. "The training, I mean. With dogs and stuff?"

"My father." Margery didn't look at me.

"What was he like?"

"He was a whiz with animals." Margery slurped from her mug. "Not so much with people."

"What do you mean?"

Margery didn't answer right away. And when she did, I could tell that she was trying to sound as though it was no big deal. Or like she didn't care. Which meant, of course, that it was. And that she still did. "I didn't grow up in a real happy house. Mostly because of my father. He was miserable, so he made sure the rest of us were, too. Think of Mr. Carder," she said, taking another slug of tea. "And then triple that."

I winced, trying to imagine someone that awful. It was impossible.

"But he was nice to the dog," Margery said. "He loved Sebastian. We called him Bash. He was a big golden retriever with sweet brown eyes. My father spent hours with him, training him, taking him for walks. Bash slept in his room every night, right at the foot of his bed. I still think Bash was the only thing in my father's life that gave him any joy. Everything else made him angry or irritable."

"Why?"

"Oh, lots of reasons. My mother died a few years after my little sister was born. He hated his job, but he was stuck taking care of my sister and me, all by himself. He'd never wanted girls. Only boys." Margery waved her hand as if swatting a fly. "Blah, blah, blah."

"How old were you when your mom died?"

"I was . . ." Margery paused, thinking back. "Fourteen? No, fifteen."

"Not too much older than me."

She shook her head. "My sister was only five."

"And you took care of her? Afterward?"

"For a while. I wasn't very good with Barbie dolls and playing dress-up." She smiled sadly. "My father wasn't, either. He ended up sending her to live with relatives. And by then, I'd saved up enough money to buy myself a bike and I hightailed it out of there."

"How old were you?"

"Sixteen," Margery said. "Almost seventeen."

"You just dropped out of school and rode your motorcycle across the country when you were sixteen years old?" I was incredulous. "What about money? How did you live?"

"I had some saved. And my mother had left me some jewelry, which I sold. It held me over for a while. When I ran out, I did odd jobs for people until I got enough money again to go a little farther. I made it all the way to Oregon that way."

I shook my head. "Man."

"I stayed in Oregon for almost ten years," Margery said. "Worked for a big logging company, cutting down trees. Oh, I loved it. It rains a lot in Oregon, so the air is different than it is here. Heavy. Dense. I remember standing in the middle of a forest once, and it started to rain. Poured, really, in sheets. Buckets and buckets of water. Everyone put their tools down and ran for the tent, but I just stood there and let it soak me to the skin. It felt so good. Like it was washing away all the stuff that I'd driven out to Oregon to try to forget."

We sat without saying anything. I wondered if that rainstorm had really washed away what she'd left behind. Or if it was still with her.

"Did you ever see your little sister again?"

"Once." Margery blinked, as if returning from somewhere far away. "When I came back from Oregon to bury our father."

A little voice in my head said, "Stop. You're being nosy, asking all these questions. Remember how you felt when Delia did it." But I ignored it. "What happened?"

"It wasn't much of a reunion." Margery stared down at her tea. "She just needed some money, really, and then she disappeared."

I got an odd feeling then. I wasn't sure what it was exactly, but it made me nervous. "Where'd she go?"

"I have no idea," Margery said slowly. "Could be anywhere." She brought her mug to her mouth and tipped it all the way back. When she lowered it again, her lower lip was trembling.

"But . . ." I struggled for the right words. "Why don't you know?"

"Because my sister is an addict," Margery said. "Which means that the only thing that matters to her is where she's going to get her next fix. She calls now and again, and promises she's staying clean so I'll wire her some cash. But she never means it." Margery pressed her lips into a thin line. "It used to break my heart, imagining her that way out there, but now I think it's better that she keeps her distance. Trying to love someone who can't be honest with you is always a no-win situation."

My heart was beating so hard in my chest that I was

sure Margery could hear it. I didn't know if the anger that had started boiling like a pot of witches' brew at the bottom of my stomach was going to burble over the edges and swallow me whole. My voice was hoarse, just slightly over a whisper. "You can stop now."

"What?" Margery looked startled.

I gritted my teeth. "I know what you're doing."

"What am I doing?"

"You're trying to make me feel bad about my mother." My voice choked on the last word. "You're trying to use your story to make me feel like I'd be better off without her!" I stood up, my hands clenched into fists.

"No." Margery's forehead creased into a map of lines. "I'm not doing that at all. I swear to you, Fred, that was not—"

"Don't you swear on anything!" I was screaming now, and I didn't care. "I know exactly what you're doing, and it's not going to work because I'm smarter than you or any judge or any stupid person at Children and Youth Services! I'll be back with my mother before any of you can blink! And you know what else? I'm glad I wrecked your stupid statue!" I shoved the chair with both hands, banging it into the table. "And if you think I'm spending one second fixing it up for you, you can guess again. I wouldn't do anything for you if you paid me ten million dollars. So get someone else to do your stupid sanding jobs, and put your dumb whatever-it-is back together yourself, because I won't. Do you hear me? I *won't!*"

Margery sat perfectly still, even as my voice cracked. And when I realized that nothing else I said was going to make her talk or even look at me, I turned and ran out of the room.

CHAPTER 31

I raced up to my bedroom and threw myself on my bed. The stars shone through the skylight overhead, and as I stared at them, I could feel some of the shaky rage inside start to leak out a little. I tried to breathe, squeezing my eyes shut as I counted to ten in my head. But I couldn't stop thinking about what Margery had said about her sister. About how she was an addict. About keeping her distance and staying away. That was just stupid. Anyone with a brain would know that creating space between people who needed each other just made things worse, not better.

Trying to love someone who can't be honest with you is always a no-win situation.

My eyes flew back open.

I jumped off the bed, grabbed my coat and boots, and yanked open my bedroom window. I had to get out of here. I didn't know where I was going to go, and I didn't know what I was going to do when I got there. The only thing I did know was that I couldn't stay here.

Not for one more second.

Dropping from the second-story window wasn't half as scary as I thought it would be. Hitting the ground, though, knocked the breath out of me, and I struggled for a moment to catch it. When I felt okay again, I ran down Margery's long driveway and made a left. Even with the streetlights overhead, it was dark as a cave. I followed the white line along the edge of the road so that I wouldn't fall into the side ditches, but even that was hard to see. And, man oh man, was it cold. It couldn't have been any more than thirty degrees, and when the wind blew, it felt even colder than that. When I finally slowed to a walk, my teeth began chattering so hard I could hear them clicking against each other. I wasn't sure if I could feel the tips of my fingers, and my toes were already starting to cramp up inside my sneakers. But I didn't care. I hugged my arms tightly around myself, ducked my head down low against my chest, and kept moving. Away from that house. Away from the voice inside that house. Away from the voice inside my head.

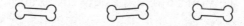

I wasn't sure how long I'd walked before I noticed suddenly that things looked different. A lot different. I slowed a bit so that I could look around. I was standing on the sidewalk of a wide, tree-lined street. A small barbershop with a red-and-blue awning sat on the right-hand corner of the intersection, and across from it was a redbrick library. Even in the dark, I could make out the words on a white banner strung across the front door: SO MANY BOOKS, SO LITTLE TIME. Libraries weren't exactly the kind of places where I hung out, but as I blew on my stiff, chapped hands I found myself wishing that I could dart inside this one. At the very least it would be warm. And out of the wind.

I couldn't imagine what time it was. There was no way of knowing how long Margery and I had talked after dinner, or how long it had been since I snuck out of her house. But it had to be late. I looked up, but there was no moon in sight. I shoved my hands in my pockets and kept walking. The wrought iron streetlamps threw long shadows on the street, and the faint smell of burning leaves lingered in the air. I passed a hardware store, a post office, and two pizza places. All dark. Shut tight and locked up for the night. I stopped for a moment when I got to the end of the block and tried to think. By now, my feet were so cold that I couldn't feel my toes. The skin on my face was numb, and when I tried to wiggle my nose, it wouldn't move. I knew the practical thing to do would be to turn around and walk back to Margery's. But I couldn't bear the thought of making that long, dark trek in the freezing cold again. I wasn't sure I'd make it. I wasn't sure my feet would make it. One more block, I told myself. I'd go one more block and if I didn't find anything open, I'd head back.

I was halfway down the next block when I heard the dull sound of knocking. At first I thought maybe my feet had actually turned into blocks of ice and were thumping against the sidewalk, but when I stood still for a moment, I heard the sound again. This time, the knocks were louder and they came in quick succession, like a drum beating. I looked up. And there, waving frantically behind a brightly lit window across the street, was Delia.

CHAPTER 32

The inside of Sweetie Pie's smelled like frosting and chocolate and warm bread, all mixed up together. It was so small that it only fit five or six tables, and three of them were already taken. The walls were covered with copper measuring cups in different sizes, each one hanging from a piece of black ribbon tied with a bow. The light hit the copper in such a way that it seemed to glow throughout the room. But the best part about Sweetie Pie's was that it was warm. Man, was it warm. I sat in the little chair opposite Delia and shoved my hands under my legs, hoping I'd be able to regain feeling in them before too long.

"Holy cannoli, Fred." She sat forward in her seat and bounced up and down a little. "I can't believe I ran into you."

I shrugged, although the truth was that I'd never been so happy to see someone in my entire life.

"How'd you get here?" Delia asked. "You didn't walk, did you?"

I nodded, staring down at the table.

"You *walked*?" Delia's eyes widened. "But that's like three or four miles! At least! And it's so cold!"

"The cold doesn't bother me," I lied. "And I just needed some air." I could feel her eyes on me and I knew she realized something had happened, that something was wrong.

"How late is it, anyway?" I asked quickly, gazing at a glass case behind her. It was filled with dozens of different pastries, some topped with sugared cherries, others decorated with green frosted leaves.

Delia pulled out her cell phone. "Nine fifteen. They close at ten, but that's how long we have anyway till my mom comes back. She's visiting some lady across the street who's making drapes for the living room."

I nodded, wondering if Margery had noticed my absence yet. Maybe she was still sitting at the kitchen table, finishing her tea. Or maybe she'd gone out to check on Toby. What would she do when she realized I wasn't there? Would she panic and call the police? Or would she wait me out? Set her heels until I came back again?

"What time do you have to be home?" Delia asked.

"Whenever."

"Does Margery know you're gone?"

"Sure."

Delia looked at me hard for a moment. "She's nice, Margery."

I nodded absentmindedly.

"Is she a friend of your mom's family or your dad's?"

"What?"

"You said she was a friend of your family's," Delia said. "Like, on your mom's side or your dad's?"

Man, she was nosy. Why couldn't she just talk about school? Or the weather? Anything but me. "My mom's."

"Where'd they meet?" Delia asked. "Did they go to college together?"

I almost laughed. Mom had barely graduated high school. She'd crossed the stage to get her diploma in a big black gown that hid her swollen belly underneath. Four months later, she'd had me. "I don't remember," I said. "But they go way back."

"Well, she's a nice lady," Delia said again. "So your mom must be, too."

"She is."

Delia nibbled on the edge of her thumb. "Maybe I'll get to meet her someday."

"Maybe." I could feel the tightness in my belly ease a little as an old guy came over, holding a notepad. He had a big white mustache and a white apron over his clothes. "Hi, Amelia Bedelia!" He grinned broadly at her. "I thought that was you over here. Who's your buddy?"

"This is Fred." Delia sat up a little straighter. "Fred, this is Lorenzo. He owns Sweetie Pie's."

"Nice to meet you, Fred." I shook Lorenzo's hand as he looked back over at Delia. "Let me guess. You two are here for the last few slices of my chocolate chip cookie pie."

Delia nodded, giggling a little. "Yes, please."

"Ice cream on top?" Lorenzo asked. "And caramel sauce?"

"Just like always," Delia said. "Thanks, Lorenzo."

"You must come here a lot," I said as Lorenzo left.

"Yeah." Delia fiddled with the edge of the votive holder. "I love it here. And Lorenzo's so nice. He knows what I like. And everything he makes is so, so, *so* delicious." She studied me for a minute, as if looking for something. "So. Are you going to tell me what happened tonight, or what? Did you and Margery have a fight?"

The strangest thing happened then, which I still can't really explain. Maybe I was tired. Or maybe everything that had just happened finally caught up to me. Whatever it was, all my anger at Margery and now at Delia for being so nosy again just sort of came and then went. And in its place, I felt nothing but sadness. Pure, silver sadness, without any anger or worry or fear mixed in with it. It was a heavy feeling, like maybe how sinking underwater might feel, and for a moment, I couldn't breathe.

Delia reached out and cupped my folded hands inside hers. "Fred?"

I nodded my head.

Her hands tightened a little bit around mine. "Can you tell me about it?"

I stared at the candle sitting on the table between us. The edges had long since melted, and the sides of it drooped. How much longer did it have, I wondered, before it burned down to nothing?

"Just try," Delia whispered.

I lifted my eyes. Delia nodded encouragingly at me, and when she did, I could feel some air coming back into my lungs. "I can't," I whispered.

"Okay." She squeezed my hands a second time. "It's okay. When you're ready, you can tell me." She nodded. "I'll be here."

I nodded okay, but I didn't mean it. I couldn't tell her why I'd yelled at Margery. And I'd never be ready to talk about Mom.

Not with her.

Not with anyone.

CHAPTER 33

After we finished our chocolate chip cookie pie, Delia's
mother drove me back to Margery's. She was a small
woman with short, streaky hair and a long nose. A large
gold ring with a red stone glittered on her right hand. She
smiled and nodded as Delia introduced me, but she
didn't say anything. I thought her eyes flicked over us in
the rearview mirror once or twice as we headed down
the street, but that was all. She stayed in the car as Delia
walked me up the front steps, and waved goodbye from
the window. I hadn't asked Delia to come in with me, but
I was kind of glad she did. There was no telling what
state Margery would be in, or what she might do when I
showed up again.

We didn't even get to the top of the steps before
Margery, dressed in a nightgown and one brown work
boot, burst out of the house. Her eyes were wild as she
grabbed me around the shoulders. "You're okay?" she
gasped. I nodded dumbly, staring at her hair, which hung

down loose around her face. It made her look a little bit like a witch. "Oh, thank God," she said. "I didn't even realize you were gone until I went in to tell you good night. I thought maybe you'd snuck out back to sit with Toby again, but when you weren't there, either . . ." She gripped me harder around the shoulders, and for a minute, I was afraid she was going to hug me. "I was just about to go down to the police station and file a report."

"In your nightgown?" Delia asked.

Margery looked startled, as if she'd just noticed Delia standing there next to me. "You've been with Delia all this time?" she asked. "That's where you went?"

Delia and I took turns telling her the story. Margery glanced at Delia's car. "Is that your mother there?"

"Yes," Delia said.

Margery walked down the steps, and as Delia and I watched from the porch, Delia's mother rolled down the window. We stood there without saying anything as they talked. Finally, Margery looked up at us. "Will you guys come over here for a minute?"

Delia and I exchanged a glance. "This could be really, really bad," Delia muttered as we made our way down the steps, "or really, really good."

I didn't know what to expect, either. It turned out, though, that Margery had asked if Delia could spend Friday here with me. "That is, if you want her to." Margery nodded at me. Delia gasped and grabbed my arm, and when I nodded and she squealed, we all laughed a little.

Even Delia's mother smiled. "I'll take that as a yes," she said. "Thank you both. I can drop her off in the morning."

After they left, I got a little nervous again. I wasn't sure if Margery was still angry with me for running off the way I had. Or maybe she'd let it go now that I was safely back.

I had just turned off the lights in my room and slid under the covers when the knock on my door came. I closed my eyes and braced myself. "Come in."

Margery opened the door. Her hands were in the pockets of her fuzzy purple robe, and she'd plaited her hair back into its usual braid. For a long moment, she just stood there, looking at me. "Do you mind if I sit down?" she asked finally, nodding toward the bed.

Oh, man. This was going to take a while. "Go ahead," I said, moving over to make room for her.

Margery eased down, taking her hands out of her pockets and folding them in her lap. The bed creaked under her weight, but she didn't seem to notice. "It frightened me, thinking you'd run off," she said quietly. "I can't remember the last time I've ever felt anything like that."

"I'm sorry," I said. "I shouldn't have done that."

She looked at me again, and her eyes squinted the way they did when she was thinking about something. "May I ask you something personal?"

I shrugged.

"You don't have to answer if you don't want to."

"Okay."

"Does your mom have an issue with drugs?"

"No." I could feel the flare inside my chest light up again. "No. She doesn't even *take* drugs."

"Okay." Margery was staring at me so hard that I had to look away.

"She takes pills," I said before I could stop myself. "But they're just normal prescriptions. You know, that people have to take for normal stuff. Like sleeping and being anxious and stuff. And they're from a doctor."

"Pills are drugs, too," Margery said, and her voice was so gentle when she said it that I felt like crying.

"I know they are, I guess. But it's not what you think. She doesn't have a problem."

"Can you tell me why she got sent to jail?"

"Because the dumb manager at her work told the police she stole some pills." I narrowed my eyes. "Which she totally didn't. She just put them in her pocket to take up front and she forgot about them. He's a jerk. He just has it out for her because she's late for work sometimes." By now, my chest was so tight that it hurt to take a breath. "Why are you asking me all of this anyway? Didn't Carmella tell you everything?"

"She told me your mother was in jail," Margery said. "But that was it. I didn't ask, and she didn't say any more."

She shrugged. "Besides, that part isn't really any of my business. You are."

I stared down at the quilt. Up until that point, I realized, I'd thought of Margery as one of the people who were Out to Get Mom. The other ones were Carmella, Mr. McCormick, all the people at the jail, and the judge who would be presiding over her hearings. But that shifted suddenly when Margery said that Mom was none of her business. And that I was the only part she cared about.

"I'm sorry for what I said earlier." I kept my eyes down. "You know, about your sister and my—" I stopped talking as Margery put a hand over mine.

"You don't have to apologize," she said. "I understand why you said those things. I probably would have said them, too, if I were in your shoes."

For some reason, that stupid crying feeling came back then. I swallowed hard over a knot in my throat and dug my thumbnail into my palm.

"You know," Margery said, "I was just so . . . *angry* that I couldn't help my sister. That she didn't want to be helped. I was even angry with my dad, who'd sort of given up on both of us before we even had a chance." She nodded. "But all that anger was starting to eat away at me. And I knew I had to do something with it, you know? Because if I didn't, I wouldn't have anything left inside." Her hand was still over mine.

"And working with the junk helped?" I asked softly.

"A lot. But it's solitary work, as I think you're starting to realize." I smiled. "And people can only do so much alone. Then a few months ago, someone at work mentioned how there was such a need for foster parents, and I went home and thought about it and I decided that I wanted to give that a go, too. That maybe if I could give a little something to a kid who carried all those big feelings around the way I did, it might help both of us."

I stared at her large hands, the way the calloused knuckles poked up under her skin like wide, dusty mushrooms. I wondered if she ever felt lonely the way I sometimes did, as if she'd been left behind somehow, or forgotten by the whole entire world.

"It's funny how certain people come into your life when they do," Margery said. "Isn't it?"

I lowered my eyes again, but I didn't answer right away. I was thinking about what Delia had said about meeting me. About how she thought maybe we had come into each other's lives for a reason. Maybe Margery and I had met for a reason, too. And even though it wasn't something I understood just yet, it made me feel a little hopeful, thinking of it.

"Yeah," I said, nodding. "It is."

CHAPTER 34

"I get that she wants you to fix it——"

"Not fix." I interrupted Delia for the second time the next morning. "Rebuild. She said she wants me to rebuild it. Into something completely my own. Whatever that means." I clapped my hands. "Come here, Toby. Come here, buddy." I grinned as he trotted over and curled up in my lap. He looked better than ever. His coat was thick and clean, and his brown eyes shone when he gazed at me.

Delia plucked a piece of metal out from the middle of the smashed structure and held it up in front of her. "I think it means you can do whatever you want. It sounds like fun."

"I think it sounds like a nightmare." I buried my nose in Toby's neck, wondering if I'd given in too easily this morning during my conversation with Margery.

"I can't force you to do anything with the sculpture," she'd said, pouring coffee into a long silver thermos, "but you're not sitting around all day, doing nothing. Especially with Delia here. I have a few more pieces that I can give each of you to sand."

"Actually, I thought I might look at the sculpture again." I kept my eyes on my bagel. I hadn't known I was going to say such a thing until it came out of my mouth. But maybe I'd try it. After all, my fits and rages weren't getting me anywhere. And it had worked for Margery. Maybe it would work for me, too.

"Okay." Margery screwed the top on the thermos and shoved it in her bag. "But I want to see that something's actually been done by the time I get home. Don't tell me you're going to work on it if you're not just to get me out of the house. You're still on suspension from school." She raised an eyebrow. "Got it?"

I nodded and rolled my eyes as she headed out the door. Man, she was tough. Fair, but tough.

"Do you have *any* idea at all what you might want to make?" Delia asked now. She was still picking at the shattered pieces of metal. "Like a person? Or a piece of furniture, maybe?" Her eyes widened. "Or a tree! How about a tree? You could use all different sorts of crazy things for the leaves. That could be really cool."

"I don't think so." I grabbed Toby's leash. "Margery said I could poke through her stuff out back, though. That might give me some ideas. Why don't we let Toby run while we look?"

"Sounds like a plan." Delia put the twisted piece of metal down on the table. "Let's go."

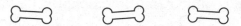

We spent the remainder of the morning pawing through Margery's junk collection. It was hard to know where to start, since there was so much of everything, and harder still to know what to take. And Delia wasn't helping. Like, at all. She spent the first ten minutes just staring at an old windmill sitting in the middle of all the junk, and shaking her head.

"This thing is incredible," she said. "It's got to be at least a hundred years old."

"Maybe." I was running my fingers over the rusted buttons on a washing machine in the far corner. Was there anything I could make out of them? I had no idea.

"I mean, where do you even find something like this?" Delia asked.

"No clue."

"Maybe Margery was out driving and saw it on some guy's farm." Delia cupped a hand around one of the blades. "You think she just went up to him and said, 'Hey, dude, can I have the top of your windmill?'"

"Probably."

Delia giggled. "Can you imagine? I wonder how she got it home. She doesn't have a truck or anything, does she?"

"I don't think so." I tried to push down my irritation. Delia talked sometimes the way people breathed—steadily and without much thought. "It doesn't really matter, though, Delia. I can't do anything with that thing anyway. It's too big. Will you look around for something else?"

"Oh, I wish you could use it." Delia moved reluctantly toward a pile of bike chains and picked one up. "It's just so cool."

"You think all this stuff is cool." I rolled my eyes and picked up an old teakettle. It had an old-fashioned spout, long and curved at the tip. Nice enough to look at, but what were you supposed to *do* with it?

"Well, it is!"

"How about that bike chain?" I nodded at the one she held in her hands. "What's so cool about that?"

Delia looked at the chain for a minute. She turned it around and studied the other side. "Okay, so maybe a bike chain isn't that cool." She put it down and moved toward the windmill again. "But *this* thing!" She ran her fingertips along the edge of one of the blades again. "I'm telling you, Fred. You've gotta do something with it. Seriously. It could be the—"

"I don't *want* to do anything with it!" I flung the teakettle across the yard. It made a dull clunking sound as it hit a pile of hubcaps and then rolled off to one side. "Geez, Delia, don't you ever *listen*?"

She stared at me with wide, unblinking eyes, as if I'd just slapped her. And then she stood up a little taller and straightened her shoulders. "You don't have to talk to me like that." Her voice was barely above a whisper, but it was as serious as I'd ever heard it. "I'm just trying to help."

"I'm sorry." I stared at the space of grass between my feet. Suddenly, I looked back up. "Delia . . ." I started.

But she was already nodding. "I did it, didn't I?"

"You totally just did it."

"Fred!" She came over and squeezed my arm. "Oh my gosh, I really did it! I totally just stood up for myself!"

I nodded, forcing myself not to pull away as she squeezed even tighter. "I knew you could." I patted her hesitantly on the back. "I knew it was in there."

By lunchtime, Delia and I had carted a bunch of different sized hubcaps, the teakettle with the long spout (which now had a dent in it), a long wide-mouthed pipe, several mounds of copper coil, a set of bicycle handlebars, a rake with a cracked handle, and, because Delia still wouldn't take no for an answer, two of the windmill blades into the shed. I wasn't any closer to figuring out what I wanted to do with any of them, but it was a start.

"Let's go eat," I said, wiping my hands on a rag. "I'm starving."

We went inside and rooted around in the refrigerator, pulling out a loaf of sourdough bread and packages of turkey and pastrami. I grabbed bottles of mustard and mayonnaise, and a glass jar of bread-and-butter pickles. Delia got to work making the sandwiches while I set out plates and napkins. We popped open two Cokes and a bag of sour-cream-and-onion potato chips and dug in. Halfway through my sandwich, the phone rang.

"Ten bucks it's Margery," I said, getting up to answer it. "I swear she knows exactly when I come inside to eat."

Delia grinned.

"Hello?"

"Hey there," Margery said. "How's everything going? Is the house still standing?"

"Funny," I said. "Everything's fine. Delia and I just came inside to eat lunch."

"Good. And I have some news. I called Mr. Carder this morning at the hospital, just to see how he was doing. He asked if I'd bring you girls in to see him."

I stopped chewing. "Mr. Carder?"

Delia raised her eyebrow.

"Yeah," Margery said. "What do you think? If you're up for it, I'll ask for permission to leave work a little early today so I can come get you."

I didn't like hospitals. They made me nervous. And the thought of going to see Mr. Carder in one made me even more anxious.

"How would we get there?" I asked. "We can't all fit on Luke Jackson."

"No," Margery conceded. "I'm going to have to borrow one of the company trucks."

"I don't know," I stalled. "I doubt if Delia would want to."

"Doubt if I would want to what?" Delia put her sandwich down.

"Why don't you ask her?" Margery said.

I sighed. "Hold on." I covered the mouthpiece with my hand as I explained the situation to Delia.

"*Yeah!*" Delia burst out. "Of course I want to go. That sounds great!"

I gave her a look that said "Really?" and "Why do you get so excited about everything?" and "Do you seriously want to go to a hospital to see a guy we barely even know whose neck is being held in place with metal bars?" She didn't seem to notice.

I pressed the phone back against my ear. "Okay, I guess."

"What's wrong?" Margery said.

I looked over at Delia, who was still grinning from ear to ear. "Nothing. It's fine."

"It'll probably be a little weird," Margery said. "But I think he just wants to thank you. You know, in person. And I'll stay there with you. I won't leave."

"All right." I felt a bit better.

"How's the sculpture going?"

"I think we found some pieces to work with. Now I just have to figure out what to do with them."

"Remember the first step," Margery said. "Stop looking at it as junk. When you learn to do that, the rest will come. I promise."

CHAPTER 35

We took Toby out for a little while after lunch and hooked him up to his leash. It was cold and the wind bit through my jacket, but I forgot about it as I watched him race up and down the yard. The fur along his back rippled and his pink tongue lolled out of his mouth. I could have sworn he was smiling. Maybe even laughing. My heart swelled, thinking of it.

Afterward, he came back in the shop without any fuss and curled up in the middle of his little blanket bed. After a few minutes, he put his head down and closed his eyes. It wasn't long before the sound of soft snoring began to fill the room.

I turned the radio on low and stared at the objects laid out on the table. Margery had said to stop looking at them as junk, but I still didn't even know what that meant. If they weren't junk, what were they?

"Margery said I'd be able to figure this out," I said finally, "but I don't have a clue where to start. Seriously, I've got nothing."

"Well, you don't have to build it today." Delia settled herself on a stool. "Let's do something else until Margery picks us up."

"We can't. She really expects me to get started at least." I fingered the edge of one of the windmill blades. "She was pretty firm about that this morning."

"We *did* get started." Delia swept an arm over the objects. "We found all these pieces and brought them in!"

I shrugged. It didn't feel like much, but she was right. It was something.

"I know." Delia's eyes gleamed as she reached into her back pocket and took out her cell phone. "Let's practice some of the Quiz Bowl questions. I'll ask you science ones. Just to see how many you can get right."

I could feel something jump inside, but I pushed it down. "Nah. I'm telling you, Delia, I really don't—"

"You scared?" She raised that one eyebrow of hers and grinned. "Huh? Worried you might not actually be Einstein?"

I cocked my head and gave her a look.

"Come on!" she said. "Just for the fun of it!" She looked down at her phone and started scrolling. "Here's the first one from last year's competition. No one got it, either. I remember. The whole audience gasped after

Marissa Maynard, who's like the smartest kid in the whole school, gave the wrong answer."

I stared at her. My nose began to twitch.

"What is the most common source of energy for human brain cells?"

I could feel my body relax. I'd learned this just last year, in Mrs. Wright's science class. "Glucose."

Delia studied the screen for a second. "Yes!" She looked back up at me. "That's right!"

I tried not to smile, but I couldn't help it. Knowing an answer that the smartest kid in another school had gotten wrong felt pretty good.

"Okay, here's another one," Delia said. "Which bone is found in the leg between the knee and the hips?"

"The femur."

Delia stared at me again. "Now you're just showing off."

I grinned. "One more."

"Okay." She scrolled through the phone again. "How many times per month does the moon orbit Earth?"

"That's too easy," I said. "Gimme another one."

"What's the answer?"

"One," I said. "Everyone knows that."

Delia blinked. "I didn't know that."

"That's why we only have one full moon a month."

"Huh," Delia said. "Okay, how about this one? What's the only bird in the world that can fly backward?"

"The hummingbird."

Delia was shaking her head. "You *are* an Einstein."

"No, I'm not," I said, although I kind of loved her for saying so. "I told you—I just really like science. I think it's interesting."

"You've gotta be on the Quiz Bowl team, Fred. I'm telling you. No one will believe how smart you are. They'll all be screaming to get you on their team."

I didn't want to get into another argument, so I changed the subject. "How about if I ask you some of the math ones?"

"Okay!" Delia's face had a way of lighting up when she was happy about something. It almost gave me the same feeling I got when I saw Toby running.

"Okay," I started. "What is seven to the third power?"

"Three hundred and forty-three," Delia answered promptly.

"Nice! Okay, how about one to the eightieth power?"

"One."

I shook my head. "Didn't know that one at all."

"That's pre-algebra," Delia said. "Have you taken that yet?"

"Nope."

"Maybe next year. Okay, two more."

"What is one-half minus one-third?"

"That's easy." Delia grinned. "One-sixth."

"Easy for you, maybe. I hate fractions."

"I hate them, too," Delia said. "But I'm still good at them. You just have to find the problem's common denominator. The trick is to look for what you do have, not what you don't."

It occurred to me that while Delia was talking about numbers, she could have been just as easily talking about people. Would it make things any easier if I tried to focus on the things I did have right now—Margery, Toby, Delia—instead of all the things I didn't? It sounded easy, but I knew it wouldn't be. Still, it was worth a shot. Because while I sort of hated to admit it, Delia's law of subtraction actually made a lot of sense.

I nodded my head. "Okay, last question. This is a long one. A fifty-pound boy is sitting four feet from the center of a seesaw. How far from the center will a forty-pound boy have to sit to achieve balance?"

Delia's forehead wrinkled. Her eyes raced back and forth across the tabletop, as if searching for the answer. "Four feet?"

I shook my head. "Five feet."

She smacked the side of the table. "Darn it! I was going to *say* five feet, too!"

"Why didn't you?"

"I don't know." She shook her head. "My math teacher, Mr. Dennis, says I have to learn to go with my gut, but I never do. I always second-guess myself."

"What do you mean, go with your gut?"

"You know. That little voice inside that pops up first before all the rest of them get in the way and make it so confusing? Mr. Dennis says that's the one that already knows the answer. And it's the one I never listen to for some reason. I always, always think it's wrong."

"I think we all do that," I said. "It's just habit, I guess."

"Yeah." Delia looked a little crestfallen. "I gotta stop, though. It's killing my math average."

I was sure that not listening to my gut was killing some part of me, too, but I didn't want to find out what.

Listening to the other voices was easy.

Delia was right: It was the first one—the one in the gut—that was the hardest to hear.

CHAPTER 36

I guess I thought that Mr. Carder would be a little out of it. I mean, his neck was broken. I'd kind of pictured him just lying there in his hospital room, glassy-eyed and mumbling. Maybe even drooling a little.

But I was wrong.

Not only was Mr. Carder awake and alert, but he knew exactly what he wanted to say to me. And he said it loudly.

"Bring 'em over!" Mr. Carder boomed when Margery announced our arrival. He flicked his fingers, motioning us closer. Margery nudged me forward, encouraging me to get near the bed. I took a few steps, but then I stopped again. Man, she wasn't kidding when she'd said that Mr. Carder's head was fastened by metal rods. What she hadn't mentioned was that the bases of the rods were stuck into his skull. Mr. Carder couldn't move his top half at all. Instead, he stared straight up at the ceiling as he spoke.

"Hi, Mr. Carder." My voice was barely above a whisper.

"Which one are you?"

"I'm Fred." Delia was close behind me, her fingers grabbing at the back of my sweater. I didn't push her away.

"Are you the one who stayed with me?" Mr. Carder blinked. "By the window?"

"Yeah. And Delia's here, too. She called the ambulance."

"Hi, Mr. Carder," Delia said behind me. "I'm glad you're okay."

"I'm not okay," Mr. Carder said to the ceiling. "My neck is broken. I don't know if I'll ever be able to walk again."

Delia and I exchanged a helpless glance. What were we supposed to say? Especially to someone like Mr. Carder who'd just said something like that?

"You're alive," Margery said. "And that's all that matters." She leaned over and patted Mr. Carder's foot, which stuck up from under the blanket like a little mountain. "There's no reason to start getting bleak about things."

"Easy for you to say." Mr. Carder's mouth tightened. "You're not looking at spending the rest of your life in a wheelchair."

"Better a wheelchair than under the ground," Margery shot back. "Now, I brought these girls over specially, like you asked. Was there something you wanted to say to them?"

Mr. Carder sniffed. His eyes roved over the ceiling, and after another moment, he cleared his throat. "I ain't never been someone who sits around and thinks about things," he said finally. "I'm a working man. Been working at the same place for the last thirty-six years. Up at dawn, home at dusk. Even on the weekends."

"You work on the weekends?" Delia asked.

"Never missed one," Mr. Carder answered. "I like to keep busy. Hate to waste time." He sighed, and when he did, it sounded as if all the air inside his chest leaked out with it. "Now all I have is time. And lying here on my back, I can't do nothing but think."

I could feel Margery watching me from the end of Mr. Carder's bed. She nodded when I glanced over at her, encouraging me to respond. "Whatcha been thinking about?" I asked, hoping that was the right question.

Mr. Carder pursed his lips and squinted his eyes, and I took a step back, sure that he was going to start barking at me. But then the hardness around his mouth softened and his eyes grew slack. "The dog, mostly."

"Toby?" I said.

"Yeah," Mr. Carder said. "Toby." He cleared his throat. "I ain't done right by him. All these years, I guess I've been so busy that I didn't really give him what he needed."

"He's doing okay, though," I said. "We gave him a

bath and cleaned him up. He's been sleeping in Margery's shed out back. We fixed him up a nice bed with blankets and stuff."

"We got him a leash, too," Delia chimed in. "So he can run around without actually running away."

"That's nice," Mr. Carder said softly. "That's real nice of you girls. And I'm obliged to you."

I wasn't sure what "obliged" meant, but I was pretty sure it was Mr. Carder's way of saying thank you. I was actually starting to relax a little bit.

But Mr. Carder wasn't finished. "You know, when I get home, he'll have to come back to me. To my house. And I don't want no fussing."

Margery flicked her eyes at him. "John?"

"That's why I wanted you to bring the girls here," Mr. Carder said. "It's all well and good that you're giving Toby some attention right now. But when I get home, he'll be coming back over to my house. He's my animal. Bottom line. And I don't want no problems."

I could feel something flare inside. "But how will you take care of him?"

"You leave that up to me."

I looked over at Margery, but she just shook her head. I bit my lip and tried to quiet the hard, mean little part of me. But it didn't work. "He won't want to go back with you," I heard myself say. "Not after how nice we've been to him."

"Fred." Margery shook her head again.

A muscle pulsed in Mr. Carder's cheek. "You don't know anything about my dog."

"I know more than you do." I talked as fast as I could, even as Margery moved toward me. "I know he likes being clean." I pulled away as Margery grabbed my arm. "And warm. I know he likes chopped-up hamburger and salami. I know he likes to run! I know he—"

"You know, from what I've heard, it sounds like Margery's been real nice to you, too." Mr. Carder's voice was tight and clipped. Margery let go of my arm. "Does that mean you're not going to want to go back to your mother when she gets out of jail?"

My mouth fell open. The floor swayed beneath my feet. I was pretty sure if Mr. Carder had sat up in bed just then and punched me in the stomach, it would not have hurt nearly as much.

"Okay, we're done here." Margery half pulled, half pushed me out of Mr. Carder's room and down the bright hallway. I tried to twist out of her grip, but it was impossible. Her hand was like a steel trap. Delia trotted behind us, trying to keep up.

"All right," I said as we made our way around the corner. "All *right*! Let go of me!"

Margery released my arm. She just stood there for a minute, breathing hard.

"You told him?" I could barely get the words out. "About *Mom*?"

Margery nodded.

"When?"

"Yesterday. When I came to see him."

"Why?" I clenched my fingers.

"I've never had anyone live in the house before," Margery said. "He just started asking questions."

"You had no right." I glared at her. "That's none of his business. That's not anyone's business!"

"You're right." Margery held my gaze. "I'm sorry, Fred."

Her apology caught me off guard. I'd expected her to give me another excuse.

"Fred." Delia touched my arm. "I know I probably shouldn't say this right now, but—"

"Please stop talking." I shrugged her hand off and glared again at Margery. "Can we just go? Now? I really need to get out of here."

"Yes." Margery nodded at Delia. "Come on. Let's go home."

CHAPTER 37

Margery didn't say anything else as we dropped Delia off and drove back to her place. I was glad for the silence, grateful even. I had nothing to say to her. I didn't know if I ever would again.

I went straight to bed when we got home and stared up at the stars through the skylight. Mr. Carder's words banged around in my head over and over again: *Margery's been real nice to you, too. Does that mean you're not going to want to go back to your mother when she gets out of jail?* What right did he have, comparing my situation to Toby's? John Carder was a mean, stupid man who didn't know anything about anybody. And Toby was just an animal that didn't know any better. Who didn't care where he was or who he was with, as long as someone was nice to him. Nothing about his situation was like mine. Nothing.

I fell asleep after a long, long time, only to be awakened again by a faint knocking. I squinted as pale light streamed down through the window. "Hey there, sleepy-head," Margery said, sticking her head in. "It's almost noon. You hungry?"

I rolled over and pulled the covers on top of my head. After another moment, I could hear the door click softly behind me. When a second knock came, it was dark again. This time, Margery walked into the room. She set a tray on the little table next to my bed and sat down. I could smell something like chicken. Maybe cooked carrots. Corn bread. My stomach growled.

"Come on, now," Margery said, shaking one of my shoulders. "You've been sleeping for almost eighteen hours. You're all caught up. It's time to eat something."

"I'm not hungry." My voice was muffled against my pillow.

"Too bad." Margery pulled the lip of my comforter down. "You need to eat anyway."

I snatched the cover back. "I don't *want* anything."

There was a pause. "Being angry at me isn't going to help anything."

I didn't answer.

Margery sat for another moment without moving. Then she picked up the tray and walked out of the room.

After a few more minutes, I heard the door open again. I threw back the covers, ready to start yelling, when Toby leaped onto the bed. He pushed his nose against my neck and made little whimpering sounds as Margery shut the door behind us. I turned and pulled the covers over my head again. "Go away," I muttered.

But Toby didn't go away. He stayed there for hours as I lay thinking about Mom and Margery and Delia and Mr. Carder. He pressed up against me, motionless as a stone, and didn't make a sound. After a long time, I turned and looked at him. He raised his head as I reached for him, and crept forward a few inches so that I could scratch the back of his neck. "You're the best friend I've ever had," I whispered. "You know that, buddy?" He licked my wrist as I petted him, and snuggled in tight along the inside of my arm, and after a while, we both fell asleep again.

I could hear voices in the kitchen the next morning, and although I still didn't want to see or talk to anyone, my stomach was so empty I felt nauseous. Toby was gone; Margery had probably come to let him outside so he could pee. I pulled on a sweatshirt and jeans and headed downstairs.

"Hey there!" Margery flipped a pancake inside a black skillet. "You hungry yet?"

I nodded and glanced over at Delia, who was sitting in one of the kitchen chairs. I sat down across from her.

"Hey," she said softly. "I hope it's okay that I'm here."

I shrugged, but my face burned, thinking of what she knew.

"Margery and I were going to take Toby over to the park and start teaching him to come when his name is called." Delia looked at me hopefully. "You want to join us?"

"Nah." I shook my head as Margery slid a blue ceramic plate with three pancakes in front of me. A pat of butter glistened on top of them, and the edges were brown and crisp. I folded the top pancake in half and shoved it in my mouth.

"Use your fork, please." Margery eyed me from the stove.

I grabbed the fork and started cutting the other two pancakes, still chewing the first.

"You want syrup?" Delia pushed the bottle over.

I nodded, dumping the thick liquid over the pancake stack.

"Slow down, now," Margery said. "You'll make yourself sick."

I forced myself to ease up, but I didn't stop eating. Margery slid two more pancakes onto my plate and four slices of bacon to go with them. I inhaled them all and sat back finally as I finished the last gulp of milk.

"Full?" Margery asked.

I nodded.

"Feel better?"

I shrugged.

Delia dragged a chunk of pancake through a puddle of syrup on her plate. "Come with us!" she pleaded. "It's not even that cold out today. Toby'll want to see you. And he'll probably listen to you more than he will to us." She glanced at Margery. "No offense."

"None taken." Margery wiped her hands on a dish-cloth, then took my plate and glass from the table. "I think Delia's right. The two of you will have much better luck with him than I will. He's much more accustomed to being around the both of you. Why don't you go take a hot shower, Fred? It's amazing what a full stomach and a clean body can do for a foggy head."

I gave her a look, but inside I'd already given in. I got up and headed for the shower.

It wasn't like I had anything better to do.

CHAPTER 38

"I'm so nervous about tomorrow I could puke," Delia said as we led Toby toward the tennis courts. Margery had told us it was a good place to teach him name recall because it was a big enough space for him to run around in, but it was also fenced in. Teaching him to come back when his name was called was the most important of all the commands, because if Toby learned it, he could keep himself out of danger. If he was racing toward a road, for example, and stopped when he heard his name called, it could prevent him from getting hit. If he got lost in the woods but heard us calling his name, he would only have to move toward our voices to find his way back out again.

"Why?" I asked.

"It's Monday," Delia answered. "We have school."

"And?"

"And that means I'll be seeing Michelle," Delia said. "You know, in science class."

I watched Toby as he raced up and down the length of the court. I wished I felt half as carefree as he seemed to be. But I could barely even look at Delia. Knowing that she knew the truth about Mom had changed everything for me. The weird thing was that I wasn't even sure why. And what was even weirder was that Delia didn't seem uncomfortable at all. If anything, it almost felt as if she wanted to be my friend more than ever. "You'll be fine," I said.

"But I really want to stand up to her!" Delia said. "And I know I did it with you, but I didn't even really think about it when that happened. It just sort of came out."

"Well, just do the same thing with her."

Delia's face fell. "That's just it, though. I don't know if I can."

"You can."

"I don't know." She started twisting her fingers. "I mean, what if I tell her to lay off, and she comes back at me? I won't know what to do and I'll stand there, looking like an idiot."

"Just take a breath and keep going." I tried not to sound annoyed, but it was getting hard, especially since Delia was using that whimper voice again. "I don't know what else to tell you, Delia. You just gotta do it."

"Yeah." Delia looked away from me and over at Toby. "I know."

"Toby!" I clapped my hands twice, the way Margery had instructed us. "Come on, Toby! Come on back now!"

Toby startled as his name was called but went back to nosing a pile of leaves in the corner of the tennis court. "Come on, Toby!" I shouted again. "Come on, boy! Time to go, now!" Toby ignored me.

"Hold up one of his treats," Delia said. "That's what Margery said, remember? Or throw it toward him and then move back a little. So he comes after it."

"I know what to do," I answered rudely, reaching inside my coat pocket. But the truth was, I'd forgotten about the treats and the fact that Margery had said that using them would be the best way to get Toby to return to us. I tossed one at him. "Come on, Toby," I said again. "Come on, now."

Toby lunged as the meat kibble bounced near him. He pounced on it and looked over at me expectantly.

"Throw another one," Delia said.

"I got it, Delia." I tossed another kibble.

Toby ate it and then stopped, looking up at me as if we were playing a game. I could feel my impatience flare again. Why wasn't he listening?

"Maybe say his name aga—" Delia started.

"I told you I got it, all right?" I turned on her. "Geez, Delia, can't you just lay off for two seconds?"

The stung look came over her face again, just as it had in Margery's backyard. I braced myself, waiting for her response.

"You don't always have to get so—" she started.

"Yes, I do!" I threw the rest of the kibbles on the ground. "And you know why? Because you're totally all over me all the time, grabbing me, pulling at me, whining and asking me questions! It's aggravating, Delia! I know you don't have friends, but that's not my problem, okay? You're just going to have to figure things out. Because I can't do it for both of us anymore, all right? I just can't. It's too much!"

Her lower lip trembled as she took my words in. I knew they had hurt her. She would probably start crying now, too, and I'd have to convince myself I didn't care about that, either.

"You're mean." Delia clenched her lower jaw. "You know that? You're mean and rude, just like Michelle Palmer. Actually, you're even worse than Michelle Palmer because she's just dumb and all she cares about is whether or not she looks good in tight jeans. But you, Fred . . ." Delia's voice quavered. "You're one of the best people I've ever met. You're smart and you're funny and you're strong. But you have this awful side that wants to hurt people because you're hurting, and you don't know what else to do with it except push it on someone else. Being mean isn't going to make you feel better. And it isn't going to fix the whole situation with you and—"

"Don't you *dare* say my mother!" I pointed a shaking finger at her.

Delia looked like she was about to cry. "I wasn't going to. I was going to say me."

Her answer made me suck my breath in.

But I didn't have a chance to respond because she turned around and walked off the tennis court without so much as a backward glance.

CHAPTER 39

I spent a long time in the shed that night, looking at all the strange pieces of junk Delia and I had selected for my sculpture. I held the copper coil in my hands and shifted it back and forth against my palms, like a Slinky. One end of it was split, and the tiny filaments poked out like strands of hair. I ran my fingers down the length of the teapot spout and rapped my knuckles against the middle of the windmill blades. They made a small, hollow sound, and Toby, who was curled up in his nest of blankets, lifted his head at the noise. I stood the old rake up, surprised that the handle was so much taller than me, and turned it upside down, studying the thick, rusted teeth on the other end. They were as wide as a man's fingers and twice as long. The seven or eight hubcaps Delia had carted in were all different sizes, and some were so grimy they looked almost black. I lay them out side by side on Margery's worktable and walked up and down the length of it. The piece closest to me had a dent in one side, as if someone had kicked it with a heavy boot. Bits of chrome gleamed on the larger ones like the bright silver scales of a fish.

Last was the set of kid's handlebars, which, unattached to the bike they had once belonged to, now looked long forgotten. A child's plaything, kicked to one side. I held them in my hands, the cool, smooth slope of them sliding against my palms. And then I placed them very gently in the middle of the table, in between the row of hubcaps. Whatever I was going to make in the next few weeks would stem from them. I didn't know why, or what they'd become, but somehow they matched how I felt, so they would be my starting point.

That much I knew.

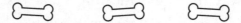

I'd counted on going back to my original plan at school on Monday, which involved keeping my head down, staying out of everyone's way, and saying as little as possible, but it didn't turn out like that. Instead, as soon as I walked in the front door, a tall, thin girl with a ring in her eyebrow made a beeline for me and slapped me on the back.

"You're Fred, right?"

"Yeah." I shrugged her off. "Who're you?"

"Bridget Dodd." She steered me toward a small group of girls standing in the hallway. "We all heard about what you did to Michelle Palmer last week. And we just wanted to say great job."

A chorus of "yeah" and "totally" swept through the group. Most of the other girls were dressed like Bridget, in T-shirts, cutoff jean shorts over ripped leggings, and Doc Martens boots. Skater girls. We'd had a group of them in my old school. They hung out on the steps after school, practicing turns and jumps on their boards.

"That chick's had it coming to her for a long time," said a short girl next to Bridget. "It's about time someone put her in her place." She tugged on one of her ponytails, which stuck out from underneath her black baseball hat. The front of her T-shirt read GRAVITY IS A TERRIBLE THING TO WASTE. I looked away, unsure how to respond.

"What'd you do, exactly?" Bridget asked.

"What do you mean?"

"You know she sprained her wrist, right?" Bridget asked.

I spotted Delia approaching the front doors. She opened one of them and walked in the building. For a split second, we locked eyes, and then she looked away again. "No, I didn't know that."

"Oh yeah," Bridget said. "It probably got twisted or something when you guys went flying over the art table. Or did you do something to her after that?"

"I don't know." Delia walked past us quickly, and I

233

glanced over as she turned the corner. Her shoulders were slumped, and her head hung down low between them. I looked back over at Bridget, who was still waiting eagerly to hear my side of the story. "I don't really remember," I said. "It all happened pretty fast. It's kind of a blur now."

Bridget nodded. "You should sit with us today at lunch." She glanced around the group as I hesitated. "I mean, if you don't have anyone to sit with. Just saying."

"Yeah, okay." I shifted my backpack along my shoulder and lifted a hand as I headed down the hall. Delia was nowhere to be seen. "Thanks. Maybe I will."

All the students in my homeroom stopped talking as soon as I walked in. Half of them were clustered around Michelle, who sat at a desk near the window. She was using her left hand, which was wrapped in an ACE bandage, to gesture wildly as she spoke, but she froze when she saw me. With her arm raised in front of her, she got up from her chair and stood there for a moment, glaring in my direction.

"I don't want any trouble," I said quickly.

"It's a little late for that." Her voice was cold. Hateful. It reminded me of Mr. Carder's. "You sprained my wrist— did you know that? I had to go to the hospital and get X-rays. Two of my tendons are *twisted*."

"I'm sorry."

"Yeah, well, my mom wants you to know that if you ever come near me again, she's going to make sure you get kicked out of this school. For good this time."

"Like I said, I don't want any more trouble."

"You better not, if you know what's good for you." Michelle sneered at me. "*Fred*. Is that really your name, by the way?"

I sat down at one of the desks and tried to ignore her.

"Lemme guess." Michelle hyena-laughed. "It was the only name your mother could spell, right?"

I could feel heat rise in my face. I wanted to smack her, to take her stupid hand and bend it in the other direction so that her wrist would break this time. I didn't care. Let them kick me out. I didn't need school. I didn't need . . .

She's just dumb. But you, Fred. You're one of the best people I've ever met. The rapid-fire thoughts began to sputter out as I heard Delia's voice in my head. *You're smart and you're funny and you're strong.*

I took a deep breath and leveled my eyes at Michelle Palmer. "I'm done playing with you." I unzipped my backpack and pulled out a blue notebook and a pencil. "Leave me alone." I opened the notebook and smoothed my hand over a blank page. I'd had an idea on the bus that morning about the sculpture. Now was as good a time as any to try sketching it out.

"*Playing?*" Michelle put a hand on her hip. "What're you, stupid? Do you seriously think I'm playing here?"

Two lines here, and another few over there. Maybe an arch over the top. Did I need to connect the middle section with anything? Maybe it would be better if I started with a base. Something like a foundation that would shore everything else up. Keep it from tipping over.

Michelle took a few steps toward me. She bent over and pressed her index finger in the middle of my notebook page. "This isn't over," she whispered. "Just so you know. This isn't even close to being over." She stood back up as the teacher walked into the room, but I could still hear her muttering under her breath. Probably about what a jerk I was and how she was going to do whatever it took to get even with me. But I wasn't worried. She couldn't win against someone who wouldn't play her game.

I looked down at my page again. The image staring back at me was rough. One side was much bigger than the other, and most of the bottom half was missing. Drawing was definitely not one of my strengths. But even with all the rough edges, it was fun to try to put all the stuff I'd gathered at Margery's together. Rearranging the shapes on paper felt like working on a puzzle or solving a math problem. If I could just focus on what I had instead of what I didn't, like Delia's law of subtraction, I had a feeling an idea for the sculpture would come to me.

I sketched more quickly, a new excitement thrumming through my fingers.

If there was an animal inside me, it was roaring a little less loudly.

It might even be stretching out now, wrapping its long tail around its haunches, resting its head down between its paws, and closing its eyes.

CHAPTER 40

But it didn't stay quiet for long.

On the way into my fourth-period math class, I tripped on my shoelace and dropped my textbook. When I stooped down to get it, a flash of army green across the hall caught my eye. It was Delia, sitting at a desk, right by the door. She had her hands folded in her lap and her head tucked down low against her chest like she was waiting for something. Or someone.

I glanced at the sign above the door: MRS. ISKRA: 7TH GRADE SCIENCE.

Michelle and Renee were walking down the hall toward me. I stood all the way back up and straightened my shoulders. Michelle waved goodbye to Renee and sneered at me as she headed into the science room. I stood there, frozen to the spot, as she walked over to Delia and jammed a finger into her shoulder.

Come on, Delia. Lift your head. Stand up.

But Delia's head sank lower as Michelle bent down close to her ear. I could only imagine the terrible things Michelle was saying.

Now, Delia! I thought to myself. *Come on! Don't just sit there and take it! Do it now!*

Delia clapped her hands over her ears and leaned away from her.

I lurched forward, ready to shove my way in between them, to tell Michelle once and for all to leave Delia alone. But just at that moment, Michelle straightened up and turned around to look at me.

If you ever come near me again, my mom is going to make sure you get kicked out of this school. For good this time.

Her eyes glittered. The small smile on her face might have been one of the ugliest things I'd ever seen.

But I skidded to a stop.

Michelle knew that being mean to Delia would get under my skin. Maybe even hurt me as much as it hurt Delia. But she also knew that I wouldn't risk getting thrown out of school by doing something about it. Because if I did, it would mean Delia would be left here all alone to fend for herself. And from the looks of things, she wasn't going to be standing up to Michelle anytime soon.

I wasn't sure what I should do about it. But maybe that wasn't important. Maybe what mattered now was that Delia knew I was still here.

And that—at least for right now—I wasn't going anywhere.

I headed straight for the science room after the bell rang, but Delia wasn't inside. I glanced up and down the hallway, catching a flash of her blond hair as she disappeared around a corner. She was running, one hand trailing along the wall, as if she might fall over otherwise. I dropped my books on the floor and ran after her.

"Delia!" I snatched her by the sleeve as I caught up to her. "Please stop. Just hold on a minute."

She shook my hand off. Her breath came in gasps, and her cheeks were pink with large white spots in the middle.

"Delia." I trotted next to her. "Come on, what're you doing? You're not going to talk to me at all now?"

"I don't . . . really have . . . anything to say."

"Can you slow down? Just for a minute? What'd Michelle say to you at the beginning of science class?"

She stopped when I said that. Her nostrils flared. "How do you know she said something to me?"

"I was across the hall. I have math with Miss Bee. I saw Michelle jab you in the shoulder and then lean over and say something in your ear. What was it?"

"Nothing." Delia started walking again.

"Delia, come on, that's not true. Tell me what she said."

"She didn't say anything. Leave me alone, Fred. I mean it."

"What's the matter with you?" I grabbed her by the elbow again, hoping she would stop walking. "Why are you acting like I'm—"

"Stop *grabbing* me!" The three words burst out of her mouth. "I told you to leave me alone!"

"There!" I stamped my foot. "Right there! You totally just got mad and stood up for yourself! Now, why can you do that—why can you yell at *me* like that and not Michelle?"

"Because you're leaving!" Delia burst out. "Okay? I don't have to care if I yell at you because you're leaving to go back to your mom in Philadelphia and I'll never see you again! But Michelle isn't going anywhere. I have to go to school with her for the next five years." Her voice quavered. "And if I get her mad, I'll have to spend the next five years trying to make it all right again. Okay? Do you get it now?"

"Delia . . ." I reached for her hand.

"No," she said, turning away from me. "This isn't about you anymore, Fred. It's about me. So just leave me alone. I'll figure it out."

I didn't say anything else as she walked away from me. Not because I didn't want to, but because there was nothing left to say.

Nothing at all.

CHAPTER 41

For the rest of that week, I sat with Bridget and the other skater girls during lunch. They were friendly enough, and whenever Michelle saw me with them, she turned around and headed in the opposite direction. I wasn't sure if she had a history with them, too, but I was glad for the space. I wasn't going to let my guard down entirely, but for now at least, it was nice to have a chance to take a breath again.

Delia was a whole other story. Every day, as I walked into math, I saw Michelle jab her in the shoulder as she walked into the science lab. Every day, Delia just ducked her head and slumped down farther in her seat. I saw her in art class, but she sat by herself in a corner of the room, far from Michelle and even farther from me, doodling on a piece of paper. I didn't see her once in the cafeteria, and when I went to look for her in the bathrooms, they were empty.

On Thursday, when she was absent from art class and there was still no sign of her in the cafeteria, I asked the skater girls about her. "Do you guys know that girl Delia?"

"Delia who?" Bridget asked through a mouthful of French fries. "I don't know anyone named Delia."

"Ardelia," I said. "Ardelia Lark."

Gina, the tiny one with the stubby blond pigtails, laughed as she leaned over the table. "You mean Lardvark?"

I stiffened. "Don't call her that."

"Everyone calls her that," Gina shot back. "She made it up."

"*She* made it up?" I repeated.

"Yeah." Gina shrugged. "At least the aardvark part. Back in fifth grade. We were all doing a project in science on African animals and she picked the aardvark. She said it sounded like her name. She even mentioned it in the essay she read in front of the class." Gina made air quotes with her fingers. " 'Ard-vark.' Ardelia Lark. Get it?"

"Yeah, but aardvark is one thing," I said. "Who added the *L* to it?"

"Three guesses," Gina said.

"Michelle?"

Gina nodded. "During gym. Same day. Michelle just walked up to her and said how perfect it was that she'd picked the aardvark to do her report on because she herself was actually a *lard*vark. And that was going to be her new nickname. *Lard*vark."

"And . . ." I opened my hands, palms up. "What'd Delia say?"

"She didn't say anything. She just laughed."

Of course she laughed, I thought to myself. When it came to Delia, there was nothing she wouldn't do to keep herself out of a frightening situation.

"Why are you asking about her anyway?" Bridget crammed a few more fries into her mouth. "Are you guys friends?"

I shouldn't have hesitated. I should have just said yes, that we were friends, that I'd shared more with Delia in the last week than I'd probably shared with anyone. Anywhere. But I didn't. Even worse, I lied through my teeth. "No, but I have art class with her, and she mentioned something about doing that big project with me. You know the one with all the bottle caps?"

"Ugh," said Gina. "Shoot me now. Like making a stupid collage out of bottle caps is going to turn me into an artist. I don't know what Mrs. Baranski is thinking."

"She wants *you* to work with her?" Bridget asked.

"Yeah." I shrugged. "And I was just wondering if you guys knew anything about her. That's all."

"She's kind of a loner," Bridget said. "At least from what I can tell. She keeps to herself."

"She skips a ton of school, too," said a girl named Lenore. Her spiky black hair stood up on top of her head like the teeth of a comb. "I think she was out half the semester last year."

"Why?" I asked.

Lenore shrugged. "I don't know. Never asked her."

But I *had* asked her.

And I knew exactly why.

On Friday, Mrs. Iskra brought up the test for the Quiz Bowl, which she was going to give next week after school. "It's a difficult test," she warned us. "But that's only because the bowl itself is difficult, and we want to make sure we have the strongest teams possible." Her eyes swept over the room as she put her hands on her hips. "Don't bother doing this if you don't have the time to study, or the motivation to win. I'm only interested in serious contenders."

I ducked my head as students began raising their hands. Mrs. Iskra nodded at each one and then wrote down their names.

"How about you, Winifred?" she asked, finishing up. "I noticed you just scored very well on the cloud and atmosphere test."

"No, thanks." My voice was barely audible.

"May I ask why?" Mrs. Iskra had a square chin that rose up into a wide, round forehead. It reminded me of a cupcake.

"It's . . . um, it isn't really my thing."

Mrs. Iskra pressed her lips together. "I'm sorry to hear that," she said. "I think you might do very well on the test."

I kept my eyes down until I was sure she was finished, and exhaled as she turned around. I wondered if Delia was still going to take the test to qualify for the math team. I wished I could ask her.

But the way things were going, even if she could, I was pretty sure she wouldn't give me an answer.

CHAPTER 42

I fell into a pretty regular routine for a while, coming home from school and taking Toby over to the park, where we'd work on his call recognition commands. Man, he was a smart dog. It didn't take him long to figure out that the words "Come, Toby!" meant that he would get a kibble. By the following week, he was coming back even without the kibble, and by the following Wednesday, Margery said I could let him run behind the house for the first time without a leash. "But don't wait too long to call him," she warned. "He's gotten used to hearing the command only inside the tennis courts. You don't want to confuse him by letting him go too far without hearing it again."

My heart was in my throat as I knelt down next to him that afternoon. I talked to him quietly, smoothing my hand over the top of his head. "I'm going to let you run now, Tobes. For real." I pointed to the empty field between Margery's house and the woods. "You can go as fast as you want out there. Run like crazy. But you gotta come back when I call you, okay? Just like we've been doing. You promise?"

Toby turned his head at the question in my voice. He whimpered a little, like he was asking me how much longer I was going to make him wait.

"Promise me, now." I stroked his head again.

He stopped whimpering and stared at me with his big, round eyes. He pushed his nose into the side of my arm.

I leaned over and kissed the bald spot on top of his head. "Okay, buddy. Here we go." He didn't notice that I'd unhooked his leash, and for a moment, he just sat there, his haunches quivering as he watched a bird swoop overhead. It wasn't until I leaned in close to his little half ear and said, "Go on, Toby, go run!" that he took off.

He streaked over the ground, his front and back feet moving so fast that they faded and then blurred altogether. I couldn't help but laugh as he darted this way and that, then stopped abruptly as something caught his attention, only to pick his head up and dash off again. He looked so happy. So free. Like the dog he was meant to be, instead of someone's property.

But it was time. I could feel my heart speed up as I dipped my fingers inside my pocket for a few kibbles. I took a deep breath and cupped my hand around my mouth. "*Come*, Toby!"

He was in the middle of another run, racing east this time, but he swerved when he heard my voice and flew back across the field. My knees buckled as I realized he was coming back to me, and I sank to the ground and caught him, all in the same movement. "Good boy, Toby!" I said. "Oh, you're such a good, good boy."

After Toby had gotten his exercise, we'd go back inside Margery's workshop, and I would do my homework while he poked around in the corners and sniffed everything he could reach. Sometimes he would lie down at the foot of my stool while I worked. Margery still wouldn't let him in the house unless she was home; she was worried that he would knock things over or start chewing on the furniture, but I didn't mind staying with him in the workshop until she got back. I preferred it, actually; the small heater warmed everything up, and it was less spooky than being alone inside the house.

After I got through my homework, I'd work on the sculpture. By now, I was pretty sure what I was going to make. Something had come to me one night while I was staring at all the different pieces spread out on the table. It was weird how it happened, because I hadn't even been thinking about it, really. I was just looking at all the pieces, and suddenly, the bicycle handles stopped being bicycle handles. The windmill blades weren't windmill blades. Even the chubby little candlestick and the hubcaps seemed to morph. For a split second, they weren't junk at all. They were part of something else. Something bigger.

I needed some help actually building the thing, of course. Especially when it came time to connect the pieces together. I begged and pleaded, but Margery wouldn't even hear of letting me try the soldering iron. "You just show me what you need soldered," she said. "And I'll do it for you. End of discussion."

She was true to her word, coming out whenever I asked her to—even at nine o'clock at night—to help my sculpture take shape. "This side to this one?" she'd ask. "And then this part over here?"

She'd make me stand behind her—far behind her—as she worked the soldering iron, and I would hold Toby, who trembled a little, as a fountain of white and red sparks sprayed the ground. The heavy mask over her face and her thick, stiff gloves made her look like an alien from a different planet, but there was nothing strange about her work. She was good at what she did. Really good. When she'd call me over to examine what she'd done, I was always amazed at how smooth the seams were, how sturdy the whole thing was becoming.

It was exciting, watching my sculpture take shape. Thrilling, really.

I just found myself wishing that Delia could see it.

A few short weeks later, the phone rang in Margery's kitchen. It was Carmella.

"We have a date, honey!" she said brightly.

"A date?" I could feel Margery's eyes on me as she stood at the stove stirring a giant pot of chicken chili. "For what?"

"For your dependency hearing," Carmella said. "The one I told you about? For you and your mother. It's been scheduled for December fifth."

I glanced at the calendar hanging on Margery's kitchen wall. Today was November 21. December fifth was only two weeks away. I was going to see Mom again in two weeks. Fourteen days. I sat down hard. "Does that mean she's out of jail?"

"Yes," Carmella said. "She was released two days ago. She has to pay a fine, and she'll be on probation for two years."

"That long?"

"She would've gotten less, but she . . ." Carmella paused. "Well, she wouldn't agree to some of the terms they set out for her."

"What do you mean?" I stared at the flowers and leaves carved into Margery's chair across the table.

"They wanted her to get help," Carmella said. "You know, go to a rehab center. But she told the judge she'd already been away from you long enough. That being apart for another month or more wouldn't do either of you any good."

"Yeah." I studied the edge of a long, trailing vine etched into the chair. Tiny leaves sprouted out from either side, and at the very bottom of it was a little flower. "Well, you know. She's right. It's hard for her. I do—I mean, we do a lot for each other."

"I know she misses you," Carmella said. "And I know you miss her. But I'm concerned, Fred. I really am."

"Why? Because she won't go to rehab? That's her choice. Besides, she doesn't even really need it. And you guys can't force her."

"Oh, I know we can't." Carmella sighed heavily. "But I'm worried that she's so against it. She wouldn't even consider it."

"Yeah? So?"

"So sometimes people who struggle with this kind of sickness will find any reason not to get better. I know it's hard to understand, honey, but deep down, they don't really want to get well."

"But she's not even sick." I could hear the edge in my voice.

"What I'm saying, Fred, is that sometimes—"

"I know what you're saying." I cut her off. "But you don't know my mother. You're just saying stuff because it's your job. Because you have to."

Carmella sighed again. "Maybe I am. And I hope I'm wrong. But I've been doing this job for a long time, honey. I do know a few things."

I pressed my lips together. Toed the floor with the tip of my sneaker.

"So," Carmella said. "December fifth. I'm sure you'll tell Margery, but please let her know that I'll be sending all the paperwork to her in the next day or so, too. Okay?"

"Yup."

"Okay." Carmella paused. "And, Fred?"

"Yeah?"

"It'll be okay," Carmella said. "Whatever happens. It'll be all right." After Carmella hung up, I sat there staring at the chair for a few long moments. The little flower at the end of the vine had funny-shaped petals; some were round and smooth while others had a more pointed shape. There was a wide curl at the bottom of the vine, too, which swooped down low like a fat comma and then disappeared behind the edge.

"You okay?" Margery asked.

I nodded.

"You might want to hang the phone back up." She set two place mats down on the table. "It doesn't work otherwise." She gave me a little grin as I glanced over at her. I stood up and put the phone on the hook.

"Carmella says she's worried about Mom," I blurted out.

"How come?"

I sat back down. "She thinks Mom doesn't really

want to get better. Because she won't go to rehab. But she's not even sick."

"They offered to send her to rehab?" Margery handed me a set of bowls and spoons and napkins.

"I guess."

"And she said no?"

"Yeah, 'cause there's nothing wrong with her."

"Did Carmella say why your mom wouldn't go?"

I set the bowls out slowly, Margery's first and then mine. "She said Mom didn't want us to be apart anymore. That we'd already been away from each other too long."

Margery set the pot of steaming chili in the middle of the table. "Do you think she's right?"

"Sure. I mean, we do need each other, you know? She's all I have. I'm all she has."

Margery nodded as she spooned a ladle of chili into my bowl. "Do you think you could go another month without seeing her?"

"What?"

"Say she did decide to go to rehab." Margery set my bowl down in front of me. "Just to get some help easing off all those pills she has to take. And say she had to stay for thirty days. Or more. Do you think you'd be all right without her?"

My eyes skittered over the carvings in the chair again. And all of a sudden, as if it had emerged from within the chair itself, I saw the fox. The very fox that Margery had told me about on my first night here. The strange-shaped flower petals weren't petals at all; they were the fox's ears. The comma swoop in the vine was the tail, smooth and fat at the base and then curving into a tip just before vanishing off to the side. I caught my breath, looking at it, and my eyes widened.

Margery grinned, watching me. "You see him, don't you?"

I nodded. "How'd you do that?"

Margery shrugged, sprinkling a handful of cheese on top of her chili. "Don't know, really. It just came to me while I was carving one night. I guess he wanted to be there."

"It's so cool," I breathed.

"Sometimes when I look at that chair, I just see the flowers and vines," Margery said. "And then other times, I'll look at it and the only thing I can see is that fox." She shrugged. "It's that way with a lot of things, don't you think?"

"What do you mean?"

"You can look at the same situation from a lot of different angles," Margery said. "Sometimes you only see the little things. The details. And sometimes all those little details come into focus. That fox—" She pointed to the chair with her spoon. "That fox reminds me to keep looking at the big picture. To keep my eyes focused on the big things. The important things."

"Like what?"

"Like just trying to be the best person I can be,"

Margery said. "Not trying to fix anyone else, or live anyone else's life." She shrugged. "It's all I can do right now. But I think it's enough." She paused, looking at me. "Do you know what I mean?"

I nodded.

"Yeah?"

"Yeah." I nodded again. "I think maybe I do."

CHAPTER 43

Every day, my sculpture grew. Three weeks after I'd started, it was already beginning to look like the image in my head. Or at least half of it was. I still had a lot more to do, but I wasn't worried. I knew what it wanted to be. And I was going to make it happen.

It always amazed me how quickly time passed when I worked in the shop. Sometimes it felt like only minutes had gone by before Margery's "time's up" knock sounded on the door, indicating that I had to come to bed. If it wasn't a school night, she'd give in to my begging and pleading and let me work for another hour or two, but during the week she was firm about my ten o'clock bedtime.

"No!" I groaned one night when the knock sounded. "I need more time!"

Margery walked in, her hands in her pockets. "Time flies when you're having fun, doesn't it?" Her eyes swept over my piece, and she nodded approvingly.

"You're really making headway on this thing. It looks good, Fred. It looks real good."

I could feel something swell inside at her words. Margery was not the type of person to hand out compliments. In fact, except for the time when she had noted how nice I'd been to Mr. Carder the night he'd gotten hurt, this might have been the first one she'd ever given me. "Thanks," I said. "I still have most of the back to do, but I think it's coming along."

"You like working out here?" Margery leaned against one of the stools.

I nodded as I began cleaning up.

"What do you like about it?" She crossed her arms, watching as I hung her tools on their hooks.

"I don't know. I've never really built anything before. It's fun."

"What's fun about it?"

I glanced at her.

She shrugged. "Just curious."

"I guess I like taking something that's inside here"— I tapped the side of my head—"and making it into something out here."

"I like that part, too." Margery paused. "It doesn't get lonely out here for you, does it?"

"No." I shook my head. "It's weird. I used to hate anywhere that was too quiet. But out here . . ." I looked around the room. "I don't know. It's a different kind of quiet. It's sort of . . . relaxing. I just like it."

"I'm glad to hear that." Margery scratched her cheek. "Still, it might be nice every once in a while to have someone to talk to."

I knew she was referring to Delia. Margery had asked about her a few times lately, and I'd brushed her off, telling her that Delia was away on a cruise with her parents.

"Yeah, well, when Delia gets back, I'll ask her over." I grabbed my coat and whistled for Toby, who bolted out of the corner and nudged my knee.

"Mr. Lark has been making his usual visits to oversee deliveries at work," Margery said gently. "He hasn't gone anywhere lately. No trips. No boats."

My face flushed. I kept my eyes down as I fastened Toby's leash to his collar.

"Fred?"

"What?"

"You want to tell me what's going on?"

"Nothing's going on."

"Then why aren't you and Delia talking?"

"I don't know."

"Yes, you do."

I bit my tongue. Why did she have to be so direct all the time? "Okay, well, I don't want to talk about it, then."

"Fair enough." Margery got up from the stool. "But if you change your mind, I'm here to listen. You want some Mexican hot chocolate before bed?"

I shook my head. "Maybe in the morning."

Margery held the door open for Toby and me. She locked it softly behind us and followed us into the house. And after I got into my pajamas and brushed my teeth, and Toby lay down at the foot of my bed, she came into my room and wished us both good night.

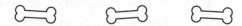

"So, are you doing that bottle cap project with Lardvark?" Gina asked the next day at lunch.

"*Don't* call her that." I pointed my spoon, which was smeared with chocolate pudding, in her direction.

"Okay, okay." Gina held her hands up, surrender-style. "Miss Touchy today. Geez. So, are you working with her or not?"

"No." I dipped my spoon back into my pudding cup, forcing myself not to look over at where Delia was sitting alone in a corner of the cafeteria. She'd been there for the last two weeks, with her back to everyone, like some kind of hermit. "I'm just going to do it by myself."

"Probably better," Bridget said. "She seems like she's in some kind of funk, lately."

"Yeah," said a girl named Lydia. "I have Spanish with her, and she's always just sitting there with her head down on the desk. She's, like, totally out of it."

"Not totally out of it," Gina said. "She scored really well on the Quiz Bowl test. I know she made the math team."

I pretended not to know what they were talking about. "The Quiz Bowl?"

"Oh, it's this whole dumb thing that they do every year for all the science and math geeks." Bridget waved her hand dismissively. "They act like they've been given the Nobel Prize or something if they win. Sometimes Mrs. Iskra keeps her team so late after school that she has to get them pizza for dinner. It's nuts."

"Delia must be pretty good at math if she made the team," I said.

"She's great at it." Bridget nodded. "Seriously. I have algebra with her this year. She kind of makes the rest of us look like idiots."

I glanced over at Delia. I thought about going over there and giving it one last try to get her to listen to me, to at least consider the possibility of making up. But then I remembered what she'd told me the last time we'd spoken. *This isn't about you anymore, Fred. It's about me. So just leave me alone. I'll figure it out.*

It wouldn't make any difference what I said anymore. Delia had made her decision. She was moving on with her life.

And I wasn't going to be a part of it.

CHAPTER 44

There was an unfamiliar blue station wagon parked in Mr. Carder's driveway when I got home from school the next day. Margery didn't recognize it, either, and I'd almost forgotten about it when a knock sounded on the door during dinner. We locked eyes across the table. Margery bit down hard on her lower lip, and I knew what was coming. But that didn't mean I had to let it come without a fight.

I stood behind her as she opened the door and squinted at a strange man dressed in a heavy black coat. He lifted his wool hat in greeting and put it back down on his head. "Hello, Miss Dawson?"

"Yes?"

"I'm Frank Carder. John Carder's son?"

"Nice to meet you," said Margery.

"You as well." Frank glanced at me. I glared at him. "My father says you've been taking care of his dog while he's laid up in the hospital."

"Yes," Margery said. Behind us, Toby gave a bark, as if he knew we were talking about him.

"I want to thank you," Frank said. "My father said he didn't ask you to do it, that you just sort of stepped in."

"Someone had to," I said before I could stop myself. "Toby wasn't being taken care of even when your dad was home."

Margery gripped my arm and tried to push me back, but I kept going. "Do you know he never let Toby come inside? Even in the winter? Even when it was freezing? And your dad hardly ever fed him. Toby was skin and—"

"*Enough!*" Margery turned all the way around, holding me by one arm. "Now, I mean it, Fred. You knew this day was coming. You've known it all along. Toby belongs to Mr. Carder. And that's the end of it."

"But it's not fair!" I shouted. "Toby has a life now! A good one! He gets to eat and run and he knows how to come when we call his name! How can you send him back? How can you make him live with someone who doesn't even care about him?"

"Excuse me." Frank cleared his throat. Margery and I looked at him. "I'm sorry this is so distressing for you," he said. "I'm not sure if either of you are aware of this, but Toby was my mother's dog."

"Your mother's?" Margery repeated.

Frank nodded. "She died ten years ago. It was a huge blow for all of us, but mostly for my father." He looked down at his shoes. "I don't think Dad recovered. He spends ridiculous hours at work and everywhere else just so he doesn't have to come home. And the poor dog . . ." His voice trailed off. "I think Toby reminds him so much of my mother that Dad can't even bear to go near him."

"I didn't know," Margery said slowly. "That explains a lot."

"I know it's difficult for you, but my father's insisted that I return with Toby tonight." He shrugged. "I think it's a good sign. Maybe he wants to give taking care of him another shot." He looked at me. "Please try to understand."

My head understood. But I wasn't sure my heart did. "So will you be helping him take care of Toby now?"

Frank nodded. "I have a job that requires me to travel a great deal, but I will make sure to come by whenever I'm home and see that Toby is being cared for. You have my word."

It was something, I told myself. And it was a hundred times better than the alternative. But I wasn't going to be able to watch Margery give Toby back. I just couldn't.

"Thank you," I said.

And then I turned around and walked upstairs.

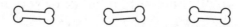

I lay on my bed listening to the muted murmuring downstairs, and for a few minutes, I let myself imagine that Margery was talking Frank out of taking Toby. Maybe she was convincing him that with all of his traveling and the work it was going to be taking care of old Mr. Carder, a pet would just be too much extra responsibility. But then I heard Toby's feet scrabbling against the hardwood floors, followed by Margery's voice as she talked to him: "Come on, sweetheart. It's okay. Mr. Carder is a nice man. It's okay."

I squeezed my eyes shut as Toby began to whimper, and I rolled over and put my pillow over my head as he began to whine. It was silent for a while, and then I heard the steady sound of Toby barking, over and over and over. It was the same plaintive sound I'd heard the day I arrived. Desperate. Frantic. The "I-know-you-can-hear-me-why-aren't-you-answering?" one.

I got up off the bed and went to the window and looked outside. Frank was leading Toby into his father's house. Toby wasn't resisting, but his head was turned toward our place. He was looking for me.

I pressed my hand against the windowpane.

Woof! Woof! Woof!

"Toby," I whispered. "Oh, Toby, I'm so sorry."

CHAPTER 45

I stayed in the shop all weekend, working on the sculpture. It was either that or go crazy thinking about how close Toby was and how much I wanted to see him. Every ten minutes or so, I entertained the idea of leapfrogging over the fence and grabbing him, but I didn't of course. With Mom's hearings coming up so soon, I wasn't about to do anything that would get me in trouble.

Margery tried to convince me that it would be different for Toby this time. Now that Frank was involved, Toby wasn't going to be left outside all night and he would be fed regularly. But who was going to give him hugs and call him a good boy? Who was going to let him off his leash so he could run through the field? And whose bed was he going to curl up in each night before he fell asleep? Not Mr. Carder's, even if he was going to try harder this time around. I was sure of it.

On Saturday I went out once to see him, after I heard him barking nonstop for over an hour. He lunged so hard

when he saw me through the fence that I thought he was
going to choke. He was attached to the metal chain
again, but he wore a new collar that was red with a blue
stripe running down the middle, and it fit okay. It didn't
seem to be bothering him, at least. Still, that chain gave
me the willies. And the way Toby was pulling on it made
it even worse.

"No, Tobes." I shook my head at him. "No jumping,
buddy. Sit." I tried to make the signal with my hands, but
it was hard to do with the fence in the way. "Sit, buddy,
okay? Just sit."

And he did. He sat down right in front of me, even
though that horrible chain stopped him from getting any
closer. It was as if he wanted to show me he remembered
all the commands we'd worked on and that he wouldn't
forget them, no matter what.

"Oh, Toby, you're such a good boy," I whispered, swal-
lowing over a pain in my throat. "You're such a sweet, good
boy."

He sat there looking at me, holding my gaze with his.
I knew he understood that I would come over if I could.
That I would change everything if only I had the chance.

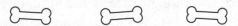

That night, I sat down and wrote a letter to Frank
Carder. I used my most impressive vocabulary and tried
to sound as polite as I could. I even double-checked my
spelling.

Dear Mr. Carder:

I appreciate you helping to take care of Toby. I know he is glad to go inside at night, and his new collar is very attractive. I hope you don't mind if I ask you one more favor. Toby's favorite thing to do is run. He loves to run more than anything in the world, especially in the fields behind our homes. If you have a few minutes at the end of the day, would you please let him off his leash so he can do that? It wouldn't have to be for very long; just so he could stretch and feel the wind in his fur. He knows his name, so all you have to do is call him when it's time to go inside, and he'll come right back.

I know he would appreciate this very much, and so would I. Thank you for considering it.

Sincerely,

Winifred (Fred) Collins

When I was finished writing, I folded the letter into thirds, put it in an envelope, and sealed it shut. I wrote MR. FRANK CARDER on the outside, just in case old Mr. Carder got to it first and thought it was for him. Then I put it in their mailbox, crossed my fingers, and got back to work.

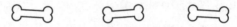

A knock on the door startled me on Sunday afternoon.

"You got a minute?" Margery stuck her head inside

the workshop. "There's something out here you might want to see."

I put down the bicycle handles and followed her outside. It was a cold, raw day. The wind blew sharply through the trees, and the sky was the color of a pearl. I wrapped my coat more tightly around me and crossed my arms over my chest.

"Look over there," Margery said, pointing across the field.

Frank Carder was standing at the edge of the field, dressed in his long black coat. His hands were shoved deep in his pockets, and he had the same wool cap on his head.

"And right . . . there." Margery grinned, pointing to another spot on the field.

It was then I saw Toby. He was streaking across the dry grass, his legs a blur of motion beneath a sea of rippling fur. Both of his ears were turned inside out from the force of his speed, and his tongue lolled out of the side of his mouth like a big pink eraser. I dropped my arms as I watched him go, and even though Margery was there, my face broke open into a grin. I couldn't help it. He looked so happy.

"All right, Toby!" Frank Carder cupped his hands around his mouth. "Let's go, boy!"

I held my breath, feeling my insides clench, but Toby, who had been moving east, swerved sharply at the sound of his name and raced back.

"You did a really good job with him, Fred," Margery said, looking over at me. "A really, really good job."

I didn't look at her, but I flushed warmly at her words. I kept my eyes on Toby as he rocketed toward Mr. Carder.

I wondered if it felt like flying, going that fast.

I hoped it did.

CHAPTER 46

"You're going to shake that knee clear off if you keep rattling it like that." Margery stood at the stove, dressed in pajamas and her purple robe. Her brown work boots made a clunking sound every time she walked across the kitchen, and I wondered if she had slippers and didn't bother to wear them, or if she just liked the feel of her work boots. Today was the morning of the dependency hearing. Margery had let me skip school. She said it was because she wouldn't be able to come get me and make it to Philadelphia on time, but I think she knew I wasn't in any mood to deal with school. Not today.

I ignored her comment and stared out the window at the side of Mr. Carder's house. I wondered what Toby was doing, if he was eating breakfast perhaps, or maybe even still sleeping. My insides felt wired with electrical currents—bolts zipping through my body one way and zapping another. And every time I thought about seeing Mom, the hairs on my arms stood up straight.

"This here's called Hunky Dory," Margery said, setting a plate in front of me. In the middle of it was something that looked like a fried egg inside a scooped-out piece of bread. "Eat up. It's going to be a long day."

But I pushed the plate away. The smell of it made me nauseous.

"Fred, I'm telling you—" Margery started, pointing at me with the spatula. But she didn't get to finish her sentence. Because just then, a gun exploded. The sound was so loud that I thought the bullet must have sailed through the window right into the kitchen. I screamed and ducked, covering my ears with my hands. Margery jumped, too, dropping her spatula.

"What the—" She turned off the flame underneath the frying pan and raced for the door, her purple robe flapping behind her. "John Carder?" I could hear her yelling across the yard. "John Carder, what in God's name are you doing?"

I stood up, ready to follow her, when I noticed something outside the window. It was Toby. He was running faster than I'd ever seen him run before. His eyes looked wild, and his tail hung halfway between his legs. He was racing down the driveway between Margery's house and Mr. Carder's, heading straight for the road.

I flew toward the door, Toby's name already rising in my throat, but I tripped on the first step and tumbled the rest of the way down the stairs. I caught myself at the bottom, landing on my hands and knees. Something that felt like a knife shot through my left arm, and for a moment, I struggled to catch my breath. But the pain was nothing compared to the way my stomach dropped when I heard the squeal of brakes up ahead, followed by a dull, permanent thud.

And then, silence.

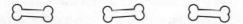

It took me less than ten seconds to make it to the end of the driveway, but it felt like I was moving in slow motion. Toby was in the middle of the road, lying perfectly still, like a forgotten sack of garbage. Off to the right, a man in a red coat got out of a shiny black car. He left his door open as he ran toward me, his eyes wide with fear.

"Is that your dog?" His voice sounded strange, as if he was calling to me from the bottom of a well.

I sank to my knees, getting as close to Toby as I could without touching him. A pool of blood had already started to seep under his head, and his eyes were glassy. He was still breathing, but with effort, as if it took his full concentration, and one of his legs was bent at an impossible angle.

I lowered my face down to his. "I'm right here, Toby." I held my hands out over him, but it was hard to know where I could put them without causing him any pain. Besides, they were shaking. I lowered them again and took another breath as a shout sounded out behind me.

"Fred!"

Margery flew in, catching me around the shoulders. "Oh no," she said. "Oh, Toby."

"Is that your dog?" the man in the red jacket said again. "I'm so sorry. I never even saw him. He just came flying out of nowhere."

"Can you still drive?" Margery asked.

"What?" The man looked bewildered.

"Can you still drive your car?" Margery repeated. "I don't have a car, and we've got to get this dog to the vet or he's going to die right here in the middle of the road. Can you take us?"

"Yeah, of course." The man started bobbing his head up and down. "Of course, of course. Come on, get in my car. I'll take you right now."

"Okay, Fred." Margery squared her shoulders. "I'll bring him to the car and put him in your lap. You get in the back seat." I nodded but stayed as close as possible to Margery as she lifted Toby and started walking. Something told me not to leave him, not for a second, that he needed to see and hear me if he was going to make it.

I could tell Margery was trying to be careful, even as Toby made a sound that was something between a whimper and a growl when she picked him up. His head went limp against her arm, and he made no effort to raise it again.

"Hey, buddy," I said, keeping my face down close to his. "We're just heading to the car. We're going to get you some help." I slid into the back seat and held out my arms. "It won't be long now," I said as Margery lowered him into my lap. I could feel him sink into me, as if he'd let go of what had spooked him in the first place, all in one big rush. I bent over his head, so close this time that my lips just barely brushed his ear. "Just hold on, little guy, okay? Hold on."

CHAPTER 47

The lady behind the desk was filing her nails when we burst in with Toby. Big, long pink nails with tiny rhinestones glued at the tips. But she dropped the file when she saw us. "Oh!" Her eyes went wide. "Oh, oh, oh! What happened?"

"He was hit by a car," Margery answered grimly. "Please get someone fast."

"Don't you worry." The lady used one of her nails to press a red button on the phone. She kept her eyes on Toby as the phone made a beeping sound. "Canine, HBC," she said, leaning into it. "Canine, HBC."

I had no idea what HBC meant, but it didn't matter. I just stayed as close to Toby as I could, whispering in his ear. He'd fallen unconscious in the car, and for a moment then, when I'd felt his body sag against mine, I was sure he was dead. Margery had turned around when I'd started yelling and had pressed her fingers against his neck. "He's still breathing," she'd said. "He's out, but he's breathing. Keep talking to him, Fred. Just keep talking."

So I had. I'd bent down low to his ear and reminded him of the first time he'd bolted, just as I was getting ready to bring him over to Margery's. And how he'd reappeared again, right on her front steps after he'd finished his run in the woods. "Like you knew," I'd whispered, barely skimming the top of his head with my fingertips. "You knew that I was waiting for you." I'd told him the story of his first bath, and how he'd learned to sit down when we did the arm signal, and about the first time I'd ever laid eyes on him—how sad I'd felt looking at his awful, scraggly appearance, but how insistent he'd been that I come near him anyway.

I was still talking to him as we stood there in the waiting room, when a door opened and a man in blue scrubs appeared, pushing a small gurney. The vet. A New York Yankees tattoo had been inked on the inside of his arm, and a mop of brown curls fell down over his eyes. He helped Margery settle Toby on the gurney, and then nodded at me. "I'm going to take him in the back and assess his injuries. Have a seat. As soon as I know what's going on, I'll come back out and tell you. It shouldn't take long."

And just like that, Toby was gone.

"Come on." Margery put her arm around me and steered me toward a line of chairs against the wall. "All we can do right now is wait."

I followed her on wooden legs but couldn't sit down. Instead, I stood by the window and stared out at the parking lot. Except for two or three cars, it was empty, a wide, vast expanse of cement. It reminded me of Toby's field. And when I thought about that, I thought about how he looked when he ran across it. How beautifully his fur rippled in the wind, and how his tongue hung out on one side. I could feel a familiar swell forming again in the back of my throat. Toby had to make it through this so he could run again. He just had to.

I turned around as the front door opened behind me. It was the man in the red coat. His face was pale as he sat down next to Margery.

"They took him?" he asked. Margery nodded. "Nothing yet, though?" She shook her head. The man lifted his hands to his mouth. His fingers trembled. We still didn't know his name. I wasn't sure it mattered.

"What made him run?" I asked Margery suddenly. "Did Mr. Carder shoot at him?"

"No." Margery shook her head. "He swore he didn't. He said he was just cleaning the gun and it went off. Poor Toby, though. He couldn't have known. He must've been terrified, hearing it go off like that, so close by."

I thought about how Toby's eyes had looked as he'd raced down the driveway. In all the time I'd known him, I'd never seen that kind of fear. Sadness, yes. Maybe even despair. But not fear. Not like that.

It was another ten minutes before the vet came back to the waiting room. We all jumped out of our chairs when we saw him, but I got to him first. "How's Toby?" I was breathless.

"I'm going to be blunt with you." The vet spoke quietly, as if measuring his words. "Toby has a fractured skull, traumatic internal injuries, and a severely broken leg."

"Is he going to make it?" I had to force myself not to grab the man's arm.

"Not without surgery," the vet explained. "And even then, he'll only have a fifty-fifty shot at survival. He's very seriously injured."

"What kind of surgery?" Margery asked.

"It'll be extensive," the vet said. "Do you have insurance?"

"No." Margery shook her head. "He's not even our dog."

"I'll pay for it," the man in the red coat blurted suddenly. "Whatever it is, I'll take care of it. Please, just try to save him."

"I didn't know he wasn't your dog," the vet said. "Technically, I shouldn't operate without the owner's permission. But if you're serious about covering the cost . . ." He glanced at the man with the red coat.

"Anything!" The man held up his hands. "Whatever it is, I'll make sure it's paid. Please, just do what you need to do."

"All right." The vet nodded at the secretary with the long pink nails. "Theresa will draw up the release forms for you. Make sure to leave your contact information, especially a cell phone number. I'll most likely be in surgery for the rest of the morning, and then Toby will have to stay with us in the recovery room through the night. But I can call you when I'm finished and let you know how he's doing."

"Call with any updates," Margery added. "Anything at all."

"No matter what it is," I interjected. "Good or bad. We just want to know."

"You got it." The vet smiled at me. "In these kinds of situations, I'm always glad to see that an animal is loved so well. You'd be amazed at how hard they fight to get back to that."

Oh, Toby, I thought to myself. *Please. Please just come back to me.*

CHAPTER 48

I was never so glad to be on the back of Margery's motorcycle as we made our way to Philadelphia a few hours later. Not only did the noise make it impossible to talk, but it also eliminated the awkward silences that not talking created.

There were too many thoughts swirling around in my head, and not enough words in the world to explain them all. It wasn't fair that to get back to someone I loved more than anyone, I'd have to leave my best friend. What if I lost them both?

It was dizzying to think about, and frightening, too. So when downtown Philadelphia loomed into view, the tips of the skyscrapers piercing the sky, I dug my fingernail into the middle of my palm and squeezed my eyes shut tight. And I didn't open them until we arrived at the courthouse.

I spotted Mom right away. She sat at the end of the hallway on a long wooden bench. Her hair had been pulled up into a clean, neat ponytail, and she was sitting the way she always did when she was thinking deeply about something, with both elbows resting on her knees, and her chin in her hands.

Margery saw her, too, and tapped me on the shoulder. "I'm going to call the secretary at the vet's office," she said. "See if she's heard anything yet." She disappeared out the door again, already pressing her cell phone to her ear.

"Fred?"

I turned back around to see Mom getting up slowly from the bench. She looked smaller than I remembered. Maybe a little bit skinnier.

"Mom!" The word stuck in my throat as I raced toward her. She caught me in a hug and squeezed me tight. I closed my eyes as her baby-powder smell drifted over me, and everything I'd been missing came rushing back to me, all at once. Home. I was home.

I held on to her tightly, burying my face in her neck. Her arms were warm around me, and she sniffled in my ear.

"Look at you!" she said finally, stepping away to hold me at arm's length. "I leave you for a month, and you're all grown up!"

"You look good, too, Mom."

"I feel good." She ran her palms up and down my arms. "I feel great, actually. I just can't wait to get you home, Fred. I've missed you so much."

"Me too." I squeezed her hands.

"Did you bring all your stuff with you?"

"What do you mean?"

"Your clothes and things." Mom glanced behind me. "We'll probably be able to walk home together after the hearing."

"Today?" I wasn't sure what the clutching sensation in my chest meant, but I tried to ignore it.

"Yes!" Mom hopped up and down a little. "I can't wait until you see your side of the bedroom, honey. I've done it all up special. It's a surprise. You're going to love it."

"Oh." I nodded uncertainly. "Wow, okay. Thanks."

"Fred?" Mom tilted her head. "What's wrong?"

"Nothing."

"Come on." Mom straightened her head again. "This is me you're talking to. What's the matter?"

I kept my eyes on the floor. There was no way to tell her I was thinking about Toby. That I wanted—no, needed—to be there to make sure he was okay. That everyone needed someone to take care of them once in a while. Dogs and kids and even grown-ups.

"Honey?" Mom reached out and grabbed my hand. "You *want* to come back home with me today, don't you?"

"Of course I do," I said too quickly. "I just . . ."

"Just what?"

I stared at the floor, trying to force the words that were climbing up the back of my throat out of my mouth.

"Fred, talk to me." Mom lifted my chin with her fingers. "Please, honey. You're scaring me by not saying anything. Please just let it out. Whatever it is."

"I was just wondering." I glanced at her quickly and then looked away again. "Do you think . . ." I stopped, biting my lip.

"Do I think what?" Mom encouraged.

I took a breath. "Do you think maybe you'd consider going to rehab first?"

Mom lowered my hand so slowly that I didn't even know she'd let go of it until it hit the front of my leg. "Who told you I needed rehab?"

"No one." I shook my head. "Well, Carmella did, actually."

"Who's Carmella?"

"The lady. You know. From Children and Youth Services. She said they'd offered it to you at your sentencing, but you said no." I fingered one of the buttons on my coat, still unable to meet her eyes. "I just . . . I mean, it's something you haven't tried before, so . . ."

"I haven't tried it before because I haven't *needed* it." Mom's voice was soft. Dangerous. "Fred, if I needed it, I'd go. I would!" She took my hand again. "Honey, I don't feel well sometimes, but it's not as bad as you think. And it's definitely not the problem everyone is making it out to be. I swear to you." She took a deep, trembling breath. "This has been the hardest month of my life, sweetheart. I'm not joking. I didn't think I was going to make it through without you."

"But you did." I lifted my eyes. "You did, Mom."

"Barely!" Her eyes filled with tears. "I was hanging on by a thread, waiting for today. For this moment." She pressed my hand with her fingers. "You're my whole world, sweetie. My everything. Please, let's go in there and tell that to the judge so we can get out of this place and go home again. Want to?"

My head moved up and down.

"Yes?" Mom bent her knees so that she was looking up at me. "Is that a yes?"

I blinked. How could I possibly tell her no? She needed me. "Yes," I said, sliding her hand inside mine. "Yes, okay."

CHAPTER 49

Carmella arrived a few minutes later. She ushered us into a big room with red carpeting and rich caramel-colored walls. A rectangular table filled up most of the space, and several chairs had been placed around it. In the middle of the table was a black phone with a wall of buttons running up and down one side. Next to the phone, lying on its side, was a tiny rubber figurine of a Smurf. I wondered why it was there, what had happened to the kid who'd left it behind.

"The judge will sit across from us," Carmella said, pointing with her finger. "You sit here on this side, Fred. And your mother will sit over there on the left." Mom did as Carmella instructed, sliding into a chair behind the table and folding her hands in her lap. She looked scared, I thought. Scared, and small, and uncertain. I reached out and grabbed her hand. She startled a little and then smiled at me, bringing my hand to her lips before letting go again.

Margery and Carmella took their seats on the other side of me. I noticed Mom glance at Margery hesitantly, but Margery didn't return the look. After another moment, a man in a black robe bustled into the room. He looked like somebody's grandfather, with white hair that stuck out from the inside of his ears, and a large, fleshy nose. I could see the top of his green tie sticking out from under his robe, which was buttoned up all the way to the top, and a gold wedding band shone on his finger.

"Have a seat, please," he said, nodding at all of us. "I'm Judge Markoff. I'll be presiding over the dependency hearing today." He opened a thin folder and scanned the papers inside. "Mrs. Rivers? Would you like to begin?"

"Yes, Judge." Carmella fingered the top button on her shirt as she went over the events of the last several weeks. She didn't leave out any details, telling Judge Markoff about my suspension from school on my first day, and how there hadn't been any issues since. I kept my eyes glued to the little Smurf as she talked. I hadn't known she'd been told about my suspension. It was almost like she was talking about someone else. A stranger.

"And you, Miss Dawson?" Judge Markoff looked at Margery as Carmella finished up. "No problems with Winifred in your home?"

"She likes to be called Fred." Margery smiled. "And no, no problems. It's been great having her. Really great."

She looked the judge straight in the eyes, her chin a sharp square.

"Terrific," said Judge Markoff. "That's what we like to hear." He shifted his eyes toward Mom. "All right, then, Miss Collins. Your turn." He glanced back down at the sheaf of papers in front of him. "It says here you were arrested for stealing pills from your workplace. And that you were given jail time because . . ." He glanced at another sheet. "Because the theft charge was your second offense?"

Second offense? The hair on the back of my neck prickled. Mom's most recent charge was her only offense. I was sure of it. There'd never been another one. I glanced over at Mom, but she was staring into her lap.

"One charge of unlawful possession, and now the theft from your workplace," Judge Markoff said, as if to jog Mom's memory. "Your actions point to a deliberate lifestyle, Miss Collins."

"But it's not the life I want to live anymore," Mom burst out. "I promise! I'm making changes. I really am."

Judge Markoff leaned back in his chair. "What kinds of changes?"

"I'm . . . I'm going to meetings," Mom said. "You know, for people who struggle with . . . with these kinds of issues. And I've been totally clean now for over a month. I haven't even wanted any of my pills. I'm through with all that. I really am." She glanced desperately in my direction. "I just want my baby back."

"And we want you to get her back," the judge said. "Believe me, reuniting you with your daughter is our primary goal here. We just have to make sure she's going back into a safe, healthy environment." He glanced at something in the papers again. "It says here that you refused in-patient rehabilitation at your recent sentencing hearing. Can you tell me why?"

"I don't need anything that drastic," Mom said. "I've got a handle on this. I really do."

"By going to your meetings?"

"Yes."

"Have you ever tried these meetings before?"

Mom dropped her eyes.

"Is that a yes, Miss Collins?"

Mom nodded.

"How many times?"

"Three," Mom whispered. "Maybe four."

"They obviously haven't worked for you in the past." Judge Markoff made a little steeple out of his hands, pressing the tips of his fingers together. "What makes you think they'll work this time?"

"I . . ." Mom floundered for words and looked over at me. "Having Fred taken away from me this time was the wake-up call I needed. I'll do whatever I need to do to make sure that never happens again."

Judge Markoff looked at Mom for a long moment. Then he turned his attention to me. "Hi, Fred."

I was staring so hard at Mom that hearing my name startled me. "Hi," I said.

"What do you think of Lancaster?"

I glanced uncertainly at Carmella, who nodded. "It's fine."

"A little different from the city, eh?"

I nodded.

"You're how old now, Fred?" Judge Markoff asked.

"Twelve."

"How do you feel about going back to live with your mom?"

I couldn't look at him. I couldn't even answer. I just nodded again.

"You seem a little hesitant." Judge Markoff's voice was so kind that it made my throat hurt. "Do you have any opinion on it at all?"

I started to shake my head and then stopped. I did have an opinion. But I was scared of what might happen if I said I did. And that made me afraid to say anything.

"Fred?" Judge Markoff said.

"I just want her to get better," I heard myself say. "That's all. I just want her to be okay."

Judge Markoff didn't say anything for a moment. When he did, his voice was softer. Deeper. "Fred, I'm going to ask you a question, and I need you to tell me the truth, no matter how difficult it might be. Have you, in the last six months, seen any other pills—aside from the prescription ones your mother takes for anxiety—at your house?"

It was here. The moment Mom had warned me about. And it was even worse than I'd imagined. My heart was beating so hard I could hear it in my ears, and a sour taste filled my mouth.

If you just wouldn't mention anything about that part. I could hear Mom's voice in the back of my head. *Because it'll change everything if you do, sweetie. Everything.*

It would change everything.

Oh, I loved her so much. More than any other person on the planet. But I was pretty sure that I couldn't fix her anymore. And I couldn't keep trying to. The only person I could keep trying to fix was me. And maybe that started by telling the truth. Even if it felt like it might kill me to do it.

"Fred?" Judge Markoff was waiting.

Someone's fingers closed around mine. Carmella. She gave them a little squeeze and then let go again.

"I've seen lots of empty bottles." The words came out in a croak. "That didn't belong to her."

"Fred!" Mom stood up, her face pale. *"Fred!"*

The terror in her eyes was too much. I covered my face with my hands and shook my head. "I'm sorry," I wailed. "Oh, Mom, I'm sorry."

"I've heard enough." Judge Markoff closed the file folder and ran his hands over the top of it. "I'm ordering the minor to stay in placement until such time as her mother seeks and completes alternative treatment." He nodded at Mom. "I'd give some serious thought to considering in-patient rehab, Miss Collins, since the meetings you've been going to don't seem to be having the needed effect on your well-being. We'll revisit this case in sixty days to determine whether or not progress has been made. In the meantime, best of luck to you both."

No one moved as Judge Markoff stood up and walked out of the room. For a long, long moment, no one said anything, either. Mom broke the stillness first. I peeked over as she shoved her purse strap onto her shoulder. She looked pale. Frightened.

"Mom."

She straightened the edges of her collar and started moving toward the door.

"Mom!" I stood up so fast that my chair fell over. She stopped. Turned around. "You'll go, right?" My voice was shaking. "To treatment? So we can be together again?"

She took a step toward me. Her gray eyes were as tired as old wool. She reached out and touched my cheek with her fingertips. "I'll call you, honey," she said softly.

And then she turned and walked out of the room.

CHAPTER 50

As the door closed behind Mom, it felt as though all the air had been sucked out of the room with her. It was hard to take a breath, harder still to stay upright. *I'll call you.* What did that mean? Would she call tonight? Tomorrow? A month from now?

"Fred?"

My insides tightened at the sound of Margery's voice. I clenched my teeth so hard I thought they might crack. This was her fault. Her doing. *She* was the one who'd put the whole crazy idea of not being able to fix Mom in my head, not me. Why had I listened to her? What had I *done?*

"Fred, are you okay?"

My fingers curled into fists as something big and black began to rise in the middle of my chest. It was like an octopus, complete with long, flailing tentacles and dark eyes, and if I hadn't been sure I had an animal inside me before, now I was certain. I could already hear the words forming in my head, the loud, terrible ones I would fire at Margery, over and over again until I was sure I had hurt her, certain she was down.

But you have this awful side that wants to hurt people because you're hurting, and you don't know what else to do with it except push it on someone else.

Delia's words rang in my ears as I turned around, and my knees went weak. The awful things that had been making their way up to my mouth seemed to evaporate off my tongue. The octopus withdrew its terrible tentacles and slithered back from where it had come, and now there was nothing left but empty space.

My knees buckled. I dropped to the floor and leaned forward, pressing my forehead against the red carpeting. I thought of Toby then and how he'd looked before we'd given him a bath, when he'd given up fighting against the hose and stood there with his head down low between his shoulders, until it was over. He'd known in that moment that it was a battle he couldn't win. No matter how much he wanted to. No matter how hard he tried.

My cries startled me, rushing out of my mouth like something pulled by unseen hands. I let them move through me. I let them come. I had no choice. The feelings were too strong. Too big. The crying turned into sobbing, and the sobbing turned into weeping. I cried and sobbed and wept so hard that Margery, who had already gotten down on her knees and was holding me by the shoulders, laid me flat on the floor and stroked my forehead.

And after a while, the tears stopped coming. My nose was stuffy and my head hurt, but something inside felt different.

Emptier.

A little bit sadder.

But stronger, too, as if all the sadness and emptiness had formed a bridge of some kind, and instead of walking under it and looking up, I was walking over it. For the first time in my life, I was standing on my own two legs, peering out at the view. Wobbly legs, for sure, but the view was wide and bright and it seemed to stretch on forever.

Carmella walked Margery and me out to the parking lot. The sun hovered behind a shelf of clouds in the distance, and the wind had stilled. Carmella buttoned her coat and then put an arm around my shoulder. "I'll check in next week," she said. "Okay?"

I nodded.

She fiddled with the row of silver earrings in her ear. "I know that was probably the hardest thing you've ever done in your life, Fred. But it was the right thing. I just want you to know how proud I am of you."

Her words felt like a hug I hadn't known I'd wanted until she gave it to me. And before I could stop myself, I reached out and hugged her back.

She held me for a moment and then let go. "You're a great kid, Fred." Her eyes were wet. "A really, really great kid."

We said our goodbyes, and Margery and I climbed onto Luke Jackson and peeled out of the parking lot. As the engine hummed and the wind whipped past us, I closed my eyes and took a deep breath. *Please, Mom,* I thought to myself. *Please find a way to get better.* I opened my eyes and looked over my shoulder one last time. The city skyline loomed behind us, small and jagged as a shipwreck. I stared at it as long as I could before it faded in the distance and disappeared from sight.

Just when we made the final turn off the highway and headed down the road to Lancaster, it began to rain. Softly at first, but then picking up speed, until pretty soon, it was coming down in slanted sheets. The wind howled behind it, sweeping over the tops of the trees in great gusts.

I held my breath, waiting for Margery to pull Luke Jackson over, but she only ducked her head a little and kept on going. She steered the bike with confidence and didn't slow down. Not once. I wondered for the second time if rain could really wash away the things you'd left behind the way Margery had said it did for her in Oregon. Maybe it could. Maybe it couldn't. Either way, it was a good thing to think about.

And after a while, I put my arms around Margery's waist, leaned in close against her back, and exhaled.

CHAPTER 51

A few hours later, the vet called Margery and told her that Toby had made it through the surgery. He was in the recovery room, where he would have to stay through the night, but if we wanted to stop by for a few minutes and see him, we could.

I wanted.

This time, the waiting room was filled with people. A woman in a yellow raincoat sat in one of the blue chairs with a cardboard box on her lap, while two little girls ran back and forth across the linoleum. An elderly man, who was petting a small black cat in his arms, sat next to the woman and frowned at the girls. Two chairs down from him was a young boy holding a white bulldog on a leash, and next to him was Delia.

"Delia!"

Everyone looked up as I said her name, and I winced. Delia got up, though, and walked over to me. "Hey," she said softly.

"Hey," I replied. "What're you doing here?"

"I hope you don't mind," Delia said. "I had to come. My dad . . ." She paused, biting her lower lip.

"Your dad?" I was confused.

She nodded. "He was the one . . . you know, who . . . who hit Toby. "

I took a step backward. "The man in the red jacket?"

She nodded. "He's going to pay for everything," she said quickly. "I hope you know that. He'll take care of all the bills. But I had to come. I just had to."

"I'm glad you're here."

"Is he okay?" Delia's blue eyes widened. "Do you know anything yet?"

"Just that he made it through the surgery." I bit my lip. "He probably won't wake up until tomorrow, but the vet said we could see him tonight." I pointed to a chair next to Margery. "You want to sit down?"

"Actually." Delia caught my sleeve. "Can we sit over here for a minute? I want to tell you some things."

"Sure."

We settled in across the room, close to the door. Delia took a deep breath. "I want to apologize first. You know, for brushing you off that day you tried to talk to me at school."

"It's okay," I said. "I get—"

"No, just let me finish," Delia said. "I guess I kind of gave up, you know? I sort of convinced myself there wasn't any point in staying friends with you, since you were going to leave. But then my dad came home from work and he told us what happened." She took a deep breath and pulled on her lip. "I know he was shaken up and he's still so worried about all of it, but oh, Fred, he talked to us. He really and truly *talked*." I thought again about the night Margery had told me that Delia said we'd met for a reason. Maybe she'd been right after all. Maybe this was another reason.

"And on the way over here," Delia went on, "I sort of realized that I was doing the same thing to you that he'd been doing to us all this time. You know, pushing you away so that I wouldn't have to deal with how awful it would be to lose you. But the thing is . . ." Her voice filled with tears. "The thing is, it's already awful. Because you're still here." She put a hand on mine. "You're right here. And I'm just wasting it. I'm wasting time I could be spending with you, playing with Toby or eating at Sweetie Pie's or practicing Quiz Bowl questions. I'm missing all of it. And I don't want to, Fred. I don't want to miss any of the time I have with you."

I covered her hand with mine. I felt lucky to know Delia. More than lucky.

Delia rubbed her eyes with the heels of her hands. "You want to hear something else?"

"Sure."

"I got in Michelle Palmer's face yesterday. I stood up and told her to leave me alone."

I gasped. "Did you really?"

Delia nodded. "Holy ravioli, Fred, you should've seen her face. I thought she was going to faint." She giggled. "I can't believe how *small* she actually is! When I stood up, I was literally looking down at her!"

"Oh, Delia." I took her hand and squeezed. "Oh, man, I'm so proud of you." We sat there for a little bit, just sort of basking in the moment. Then I turned my head. "I have some news, too."

Delia raised that one eyebrow of hers. "Yeah?"

"I'm not going back to Philadelphia. At least not yet." I nodded. "My mom still has to figure some things out."

Delia sucked in her breath. "Are you okay with that?"

"I'm worried," I said after a minute. "You know, that she won't."

"That must be scary." Delia paused. "But I bet you she will. And until she does, you have Margery. And you have me. We'll help you through it, Fred. Promise."

I squeezed her hand again. My heart was too full to say anything else.

"There's one more thing," Delia said.

She didn't have a chance to finish, because just then the door opened and the vet appeared. Margery, Delia, and I followed him down a long, brightly lit hallway. His curls were even messier than before, and there were dark circles under his eyes.

"It's still touch and go for the next twenty-four hours," he said. "But I'm very happy with Toby's vital signs. They're really strong, which is promising." He paused outside of an exam room and put his hand on the knob. "I do have to warn you, though. We weren't able to save his leg."

Toby lay on a gurney in the middle of the small, dimly lit room. His eyes were closed, and a thin plastic tube snaked out of his mouth, which hung open slightly. An enormous white cloth covered his right side, just at the front where his leg had been.

I bent over him and touched the tip of his little half ear with my finger. My hand was shaking. "Hi, Tobes," I whispered. "Hi, buddy. You made it, you know that? You made it all the way through."

He moved his head slightly, and I knew that he'd heard me. A thump sounded at the other end of the table and Margery grinned, pointing. Toby lifted his tail again and let it fall. I could feel the breath I'd been holding release itself as I stroked his ear again. He was back. He was banged up a little, but he was still here. He was still Toby.

"What was the one more thing?" I asked Delia the next day as her mother drove us home. Toby lay in his crate in between us, and Margery sat up front in the passenger seat.

"What?" Delia turned to look at me.

"Yesterday, in the waiting room," I reminded her. "You said there was one more thing you had to—"

"Oh!" Delia smacked her forehead with her palm. "I totally forgot. Mrs. Iskra came up to me at school yesterday and said that Marissa Maynard is in the hospital with double pneumonia."

"And?"

"And she's like the best member of the science team this year for the Quiz Bowl," Delia said. "She's out. She's not going to be able to participate at all."

"What's that got to do with me?"

"Mrs. Iskra said that your grades have been so good that she would waive the whole test-taking part if you would just consider joining."

Margery turned around in her seat. "What's this I hear about good grades?"

I blushed. "Our crazy science teacher wants me to join her team for the Quiz Bowl. She's just exaggerating so I'll do it."

"She's *not* exaggerating!" Delia's blue eyes were wide. "She was totally serious, Fred. I mean it. She wouldn't waste her time on someone she really didn't believe in. She believes in you." Her voice was soft. "And so do I."

"When's the Quiz Bowl?" Margery asked.

"Two more weeks," Delia said. "Right before Christmas."

Margery looked at me. "Why don't you do it? Just for fun?"

I opened my mouth to object. And then I shut it again. Why shouldn't I do it? I had the time now. I had someone to practice and study with. And I had a shot. It would be a little bit like reclaiming the Science Jeopardy game back at my old school.

Except that this time, maybe I could win it.

CHAPTER 52

"I honestly can't remember the last time I was this excited to see something." Margery's eyes danced as she stood across the worktable. "How long are you going to make us wait, Fred? You're killing me."

"I agree!" Delia laughed. "Come on, Fred! I'm dying to see it!"

"Hold on," I murmured, sliding my fingers under the edge of the tarp again. I wanted to get it just right so that when I finally snapped it off, the plastic material would slide cleanly away from the sculpture without catching on anything. I didn't want it to snag against any of the parts that stuck out on the sides, or worse, pull the whole thing down by accident. "How about Toby? Is he ready? Toby, you ready, buddy?"

He was in his little bed, surrounded by a pile of soft blankets, but he lifted his head at the sound of my voice and perked up his ears. Sometimes, when I looked at him quickly, I still forgot that one of his legs was missing, or that now it took him twice as long to stand up. He'd been home for two weeks, but he still struggled trying to find his center of balance. He fell over a lot, and sometimes, if he was too tired, he wouldn't get back up right away. Until he did. That was the thing about Toby. His leg might have been gone, but his determination was not. He was a fighter. Nothing was going to hold him down for long.

Sometimes I still forgot that he was ours now, too. For real. When Mr. Carder got the news about Toby's new handicap, he sort of threw in the towel. Margery went over to talk to him about it, and he told her it was hard enough being stuck in a wheelchair himself; he didn't have the time or energy to worry about another cripple. My temper had flared when she told me that. She said she asked Mr. Carder if we could keep Toby, and he was quiet for a long time. Finally, he nodded.

"Probably for the best," he said gruffly. " 'Sides, we both know that dog was hers the first night she came out with that bowl of beef stew."

Mr. Carder was still a mean, grumpy old man. But he'd given me Toby. Maybe deep down he knew Toby had given me his heart. And that I had given him mine.

Together, we'd do whatever we could to keep them safe.

"You ready, buddy?" I asked a third time. Toby barked once in response, and I turned back to the tarp. My heart was beating like a drum, and my palms were sweaty. I knew no one here would laugh at what they were about to see. No one would criticize, or point out the joints that weren't quite smoothly attached. It was even okay if they didn't really understand the meaning behind the sculpture, or why I'd picked this design instead of something else. That was just for me, something I'd keep in a little pocket of my heart for a long, long time. But I did want them to like it. More than anything, I wanted two of the most important people in my life to think I'd made something beautiful. That it was enough.

I gripped the edges of the tarp. "One, two, three!" With a snap and a whoosh, the plastic material slid to the floor.

"Oh!" Delia gasped, bringing her hands to her mouth.

I stared at the structure towering before us, the wide, smooth windmill blades positioned neatly on either side, each one supported by one arm of the bicycle handles beneath, like metal bones. It was easy to spot the rake; it stuck out right in front, stretching its neck for takeoff. I'd chosen two enormous hubcaps for the eyes and used the rest to fill in the body. They glittered and shone in the light, like sun dappling the trees, and then tapered off into a tail.

"It's a bird." Margery was walking toward it slowly, taking it in. Her eyes were wide, her voice wondrous. "Good Lord, girl, you went and made yourself a bird." She kept walking, dipping down at one point to look beneath it, and then continuing on. "It's exquisite, Fred. It's just spectacular."

It wasn't hard to hear the pride in her voice, and my cheeks felt warm. I didn't know if I'd ever tell either of them about that night in the Philadelphia apartment. Or that I hadn't been able to stop thinking about that little brown bird ever since I'd arrived at Margery's. There was something about the way it had stayed in the kitchen all night long—with the window open wide—before finally stretching its wings and taking off. It was a little like me, I thought. I'd held on for as long as I could inside that apartment. I really and truly had.

Until I couldn't anymore. Until I'd stretched my wings finally and flown through that window, too.

"Fred, it's so cool!" Delia said. "I can't believe you made it. I mean, I can believe it of course, but I . . . Holy ravioli, it's just so good!"

Toby barked three times, as if agreeing with her.

I felt warm and good and happy inside, which was something I hadn't felt in a long time. Something I hadn't been sure I'd ever feel again.

Mom was my first family. The one who, for as long as I lived, would belong to me. And she would come back to me when she was ready. When she was better. I was certain of it.

Until she did, I would be here with my bird and my dog and Margery and Delia.

For as long as I needed to be.

A NOTE FROM THE AUTHOR

This book deals with some heavy stuff.

And that's because life can throw heavy stuff at us. Sometimes it's so heavy that we can't even lift it, or figure out how to carry it while going to school and hanging out with our friends and pretending that nothing's wrong.

And when that heavy stuff involves our parents, things can get even trickier. Parents are the ones who bring us into this world and take care of us, especially when we get sick. They put dinner on the table and tuck us in at night and teach us how to tie our shoes. They are supposed to have all the answers.

Except that sometimes they don't. Sometimes they have problems—like drug or alcohol abuse—that can be very hard to understand and feel too big to handle on our own. That's what Fred realizes in this book. Her mom's addiction to prescription pain pills affects them both very deeply, but it's not a problem Fred can fix by keeping it secret.

I wrote this book because I want anyone who is struggling with the really heavy stuff to remember that it's okay to ask for help. You don't have to feel embarrassed or ashamed. Being honest about a parent's flaws doesn't make you a bad person. It doesn't make your mom or dad a bad person, either. Talking about the heavy stuff is a way to share the load, so we don't have to carry it all on our own.

If something is getting too heavy to carry, reach out to someone. There are people out there who can give you what your parents might not be able to right now. Talk to teachers, school counselors, or other family members who are willing to listen. If you are honest with them, they can help you.

Because sometimes your family is more than just the people you were born to; it can also become the people you choose.

ACKNOWLEDGMENTS

My gratitude is boundless.

To Stacey Glick, for her unfailing faith in me, and sky-high optimism. It's such a joy to work with you.

To Jenne Abramowitz, who has surpassed all editorial responsibilities by becoming a true and lasting friend. You work magic with words and hearts, and I am forever grateful.

To Janel McCormick and Dave Cooper, who worked tirelessly trying to restore the last seventy-two pages of this manuscript after I accidentally deleted them, and to Lisa Iskra, who assured me that the new pages I would have to write would be better than the originals.

To Nancy Sanderson, always.

And to my children, my angels, the loves of my life. None of this would mean anything without you.

ABOUT THE AUTHOR

Cecilia Galante is the author of books for children, teens, and adults. Her first novel, *The Patron Saint of Butterflies*, won a NAIBA Book of the Year Award and was an Oprah's Book Club Teen Reading Selection, a Book Sense Pick, and a Bank Street Best Children's Book of the Year. In addition to teaching eighth-grade English, Cecilia also teaches fiction writing at Wilkes University's graduate creative writing program. She lives in Kingston, Pennsylvania.